CALI MANN & FREYA BLACK

Called

Hell-Baited Wolves

First published by Thornfire Publishing Co. 2020

Copyright © 2020 by Cali Mann & Freya Black

This novel is entirely a work of fiction. The names, characters and incidents portrayed in it are the work of the author's imagination. Any resemblance to actual persons, living or dead, events or localities is entirely coincidental.

First edition

Editing by S.B. Editing
Cover art by Paradise Cover Design

This book was professionally typeset on Reedsy.
Find out more at reedsy.com

Contents

1

Del

I paced the multicolored shag rug, a nerve in my cheek twitching in rhythm to my steps.

Tarzi settled into her plush armchair. My friend's fingernails were dirty from gardening, weeding and "fueling her inner peace". Sadly, it didn't work that way for me. She'd only had to take one look at me on her doorstep to hurry me inside. She liked to tend to me, too, and I needed it today.

She peered at me over her cup of chamomile tea. "Del, you're hungry."

"I know," I muttered. I couldn't sit. My nerves were jittery and my skin itched. My eyes darted to my friend, and I wished I could soak up her inner calm.

"You can't deny your nature," Tarzi said.

"I know."

She made it sound so reasonable, but it wasn't that simple. I scrunched my nose, gazing through the window into her perfectly manicured garden. My friend liked things orderly, but I wasn't sure even she could straighten my tangled nest of worries.

"But there's Amma . . ." I'd avoided feeding around her since we moved out of our mother's place, catching a man here or there takeaway style. One man at a time wasn't enough to curb my succubus hunger, but my younger sister hadn't come into her powers yet. She was too young for me to feed around her like my mother had with me. The idea of bringing men back to our house . . . I cringed. I'd be just like our mother, throwing our succubus nature at Amma too soon. I twisted my hands together. "I don't want charmed men around her. What if one of them latches onto her?"

Tarzi sighed, her green eyes dipping toward her drink.

I crossed my arms and forced my body to a stop. I had to think about this rationally. It wouldn't do Amma any good for me to be starved and angry either.

"No, it wouldn't," Tarzi said.

My eyes met my friend's. "Did I say that out loud?"

Tarzi smiled but didn't answer, pulling her sea-green shawl closer around herself.

"You should have a party," Tarzi said, sipping her tea.

The steam swirled over her face, highlighting her thin nose and porcelain features. She was as beautiful as a doll, but like the rest of us, just underneath her skin, darkness simmered.

That was the life of a demon. We might not be the horrors of human mythology, but our powers were born in darkness. They weren't easy to live with or to use, and yet we had to in order to survive.

I dug my fingers into my arms. I'd been a succubus my whole life. I'd grown up with my mother and her endless rounds of sexualized parties. I should be used to this life by now. Instead, I'd left at my first opportunity and had taken my little sister with me. I could leave home, but I couldn't escape my nature. My need to feed.

I scowled. "Fine. But it'll be as far away from Amma as I can get."

Tarzi shook her head. "No, Del. You need to have it at home where she can start to feel the power working."

"No," I said. Images of my mother's debauchery flickered through my head.

"She needs to start understanding her powers, and the only way she can do that is through you."

"She's still young," I insisted, my jaw clenching.

Tarzi raised an eyebrow. "Not that young."

"I just want to protect her."

"Of course you do," Tarzi said. "But if you don't show her how to use her powers safely and properly, you're harming her more than your mother ever did you."

I sighed. There was truth in that. I hated the idea, but I could feel my hunger rolling under my skin. I was as frazzled as a junkie. "She doesn't need to come to the party. Not yet."

A smile crossed Tarzi's face. "No, she just needs to be in the same house."

I pressed my lips together, wanting to argue, but I couldn't go on like this. It wouldn't do me or Amma any good.

"Go home," Tarzi said. "I'll have your guests waiting for you by the time you walk in the door."

I blinked. "You'll round them up?"

She nodded. "You don't have to do anything but be there and let your succubus feed."

"Okay," I said, walking toward the door. I looked through the window at the lilies growing on Tarzi's doorstep and swung back to say, "Thank you."

The demon of nightmares beamed at me.

* * *

That was a year ago today. I shook my head. How time changed things and yet nothing at all. I'd gotten used to having succubus parties with my sister in the house—behind a firmly closed door up two sets of stairs.

3

As usual, everything in the basement was placed to make this feel like a real party. Cushions and chairs were grouped in inviting nooks, and there were drinks and snacks laid out on tables along the wall. The music from the live band thrummed through me as the bourbon ran silky smooth through my veins. I could almost forget why I was here and what I needed to do.

Rolling my hips, I trailed a hand down the tight muscles of the men on either side of me. I threw my head back, gazing at the ceiling, my legs unsteady beneath me, my eyes gaining the afterimage of the bright lights. But through that, I watched the painted wooden stars I'd hung among the lights turn in the draught from the open window and when the door opened and shut. I'd hung them for myself, not for the demons in my thrall. My sister laughed at the stars' rough homemade appearance, but I liked them. I had made them, and they reminded me there was more to life than my succubus powers.

I shook my head. *I need to feed.*

Tonight's men were watching me with varying degrees of intensity. Their eyes were glazed; a film coated their pupils. My damned uncontrollable compulsion, courtesy of my succubus mother. My heart squeezed with an outpouring of bitterness, like the juice from a bad orange.

I pushed the men's hands away and shoved through the haze of pheromones and salivating men to the drinks table. These days I needed to be far more drunk to truly enjoy that kind of mindless attention. The joy I'd taken in my power over men lost its shine when I hit my twenties. And I desperately needed a night off from worrying about what the men really thought and whether my powers would ever feel fun and new again. Craving a man's genuine attention, free of my power's influence, was pointless. Mother had more than proven over the years that men came and went and only stayed for our power.

Ice cubes clinked against my glass tumbler, popping as I poured bourbon over them. I savored the cool glass and the caramel taste. I closed my eyes, shutting out the onslaught of the party.

My mind strayed back to the weird dreams about sexy humans I'd been having lately. I'd not thought much about humans, though our world lay alongside theirs—close but not touching. I'd heard the stories, of course, that humans believed our world to be a place of punishment for them. But no, there weren't any humans in Hell, none that lived, anyway. And demons didn't go to the human world, unless by force. There were rare tales of demons losing their icons before being summoned and forced to do some human's bidding.

I shook myself. My dreams were of three sexy human men—at least I thought they were human—who saw me for who I was. That's how I knew they were pure imagination. No man ever looked at me with less than succubus-struck fascination. There was no escaping what I was.

A few meters away, a blue-skinned demon stood with his back to me. I frowned. That never happened. He must have more resistance to my charms than most, and he was greeting men and whispering in their ears.

Lucky him. He had my full attention.

He clasped the hands of a dozen men and exchanged words or gold. He was playing the party for tricks. But what kind? Curiosity thrummed through me like a pulse, and I followed it.

A dark swirl tattoo ran down his upper arm, marking him as a seer. I frowned. I didn't usually see his kind in this part of town. Most demons stayed among their own, clustering in guilds and communities . . . well, except for the underlings, the service demons—damn things were always underfoot.

In these heels, I was only an inch or two shorter than the seer. And I knew he felt me waiting behind him. His hands twitched around his latest target. When they were done, he turned to face me.

I raised my glass. "Good night?"

His dark brown eyes narrowed, but he licked his pale lips. "Business is good."

"I'm sure it is. Care to tell why you think you should find clients at my party?" In my experience, most seers were conmen, using the draw of their supposed skills to make money off fools.

"Many of these men are my regulars, drawn away to satisfy your desires tonight."

I tapped my finger against my lips. "And you? Are you here to fulfill my desires?"

"Perhaps . . ." He took my hand and froze, a film dropping over his eyes. They turned white, and he squeezed my fingers hard. His lips moved, but no sound came out.

And then the film disappeared; his dark gaze focused on me again. Only this time it was clear, unclouded by my own compulsion. His powers had broken through mine.

"Your icon was stolen," he said.

I gaped at him. I'd never seen anything pierce my natural compulsion, even for a moment. Hope flashed through me. Could I replicate that, create some kind of immunity?

But then his words broke through my thoughts. I blew out my breath and laughed, short and sharp. "Is this what you do? Convince your marks—sorry, clients—that their icons are missing, that only you can find them? It won't work on me. Mine's right here."

I pulled my necklace out of my cleavage by its cord. The suggestively carved female figure dangled under his nose. I expected his face to crumple because I'd ruined his ploy to extort money from me. But strangely, he didn't even blink.

I braced for trouble, looking all around, but saw nothing other than the usual attention of men. He didn't seem to have a partner prepared to take my icon from me and compel me to do his bidding. I shuddered. The thought of that was like frostbite over my insides. It was bad enough having all this endless attention, but being forced to do something for them, controlled?

"I'm a seer. What I see is true." He leaned away from me, shaking his head. He was very calm, but his forehead shone in the lights, sweaty. "It's not that icon."

I frowned. Only demons with parents from different demon bloodlines had more than one icon, and my mother had always insisted I was all succubus.

"You're a scam. Just admit it."

He licked his dry lips and slowly shook his head. "That is what I saw."

I gritted my teeth, dug my nails into the man's arm, and dragged him to the biggest, most muscular man I could find.

I smiled sweetly at the demon version of Hercules. "Please could you escort this man off my property?"

His lips curled into a slow smile. "It'd be my pleasure."

And, oh, how his eyes told me that wouldn't be his only pleasure if he had his way, but he'd have to wait his turn. I bit my lip. His turn. How did I end up like this?

"Please, go."

He nodded and sobered as he pulled his charge from the room. The compulsion should last long enough to get rid of the seer, but Hercules might not come back.

I gripped my icon, feeling the grooves under my fingers. I was safe. I was in control. I didn't need to worry about that man's hare-brained schemes.

"I saw you in chains, Del!" the seer called.

The Hercules-sized demon slammed the door, shutting them off from me, but my fingers trembled around my icon even so. The stories of demons returning from a summoning broken and used up ran through my mind. That's all they were, though—old tales. And my icon was here.

A black-haired bad boy caught my arm. "I do love it when you throw my competition out."

I snorted. "He wasn't competition."

"Well, I'm glad to hear you say so. Shall we get rid of the rest of them and do the things we spoke about?" His eyelids lowered as he took me in, his voice a low burr, his thick eyelashes damned sexy.

I let myself fall into those eyes until a high girl's voice pierced my distraction.

"Get off me!" she cried.

I cursed, my heart beating wildly as I ran toward my sister's cries. Men were crowded around her by the time I got there, a few sizing up the demon who'd snatched her arm.

"Get off her now," I said, my eyes drilling into the maggot who dared touch my kin. He backed away, hands in the air.

From behind me, a low, sultry voice said, "It's fine."

I spun, scowling at Prax. I knew that honey-coated voice and—my eyes flicked over him—those blond curls and broad shoulders any-where—my ex. His incubus powers stole over me, urging me to relax.

"It's fine," Prax repeated, grinning.

"It's not," I growled, shaking off his allure.

"Del . . ." my sister begged.

I turned back to Amma. Her eyes brimmed with tears. None of this was her damned fault.

"I don't care who it was. Everyone, leave!" I glared especially hard at the two men I'd marked for my bed tonight, knowing they were the furthest under my compulsion from all those touches and kisses.

But Prax was the stubborn one. As everyone else filtered out my apartment door, he draped his arm over my shoulder, like I was a damned hanger.

"'Everyone' means you, too."

His wavy blond hair hadn't flattened in the heat of my basement. It still looked perfect, unlike all those times I'd run my hands through it.

I gritted my teeth as the memories flushed through me. The bastard didn't deserve me thinking about him that way.

"Del, come on. I thought you'd want to greet me."

Stiffly, I shook my head. "No."

His intoxicating scent wafted to me from his casually laid arm. Like smoke and ivy, binding around my lungs. I *had* to go and date an incubus, the male version of my kind. I must have wanted to torture myself. Through him, I knew just how hard it was to resist our kind's charms. And how little sex with us could mean.

"Please. I need to talk to Amma."

An inch at a time, he removed his arm, gave me a sweeping bow, and left. A smirk was on his face the whole time. *Bastard.*

I took a long, deep breath, trying to ignore his lingering scent. Clawing myself out from under my attraction was like coming up for a breath in flooded caves. Almost impossible. But for my sister, I tore the attraction to shreds.

Jaw tight, I took her hands. They shook slightly, clammy, and she wouldn't look me in the eyes. Something had happened. Something bad. Rage burned my throat. Whoever did this to her, broke her joyful spirit, would hurt for this.

"What happened, Amma?"

Her lip trembled. "I can't." Her voice wavered.

I tightened my grip on her hands. "Did someone say something? Touch you?"

She lowered her eyes.

"Tell me."

My tone must have been harsher than I intended because she winced. Her eyes darted up to mine. "The second thing."

Dammit. I bit my tongue. "Why did you come to the basement?"

She shook her head. "I heard my favorite song. I just wanted to have fun."

Damn it, she'd felt left out, and I'd just made her feel worse by chiding her. I dropped her hands and stroked her cheek.

"I think it's time I told you why you're safer in your room." The words came out so choked. But it was time. She was already drawing men to her and her powers would only grow from now.

Her chin jutted up. "Good. I want to know."

I bit my lip. She was still so slim and bony, barely into her teens. She hadn't fully matured yet, but her powers didn't care about that.

"Amma, we're succubi."

"Succubi?"

Her blonde hair was the same shade as mine, but it was tied behind her head in a braid. Her nose lifted at the tip in the slightest point. She was still so young. I hadn't wanted to have this conversation yet.

"Yes."

Amma crossed her arms over her chest. She knew the basics of the common demon species, and I'd made sure succubus information was in there, but experiencing it was different. I could see the struggle to believe it in the tightness of her stance.

Her eyes drifted toward the empty room beyond us. "That's why you hold all these parties, why only men come?"

"Yes."

"Why wouldn't you tell me before? I'm not a child." Her stare was almost accusing, though tears lingered in her eyes.

I sighed out my breath. I knew this brave front; I'd used it a time or two myself over the years.

She sucked air through her teeth, blinking rapidly. "Succubi."

"Yes," I repeated, trying to just be present for her as she worked through it.

"I . . . it . . . makes a lot of sense." She frowned, looking me up and down with fresh eyes. Then her gaze went to the empty party room. "Will I be the same as you? Will I need to have parties like this?"

I held her gaze. "You'll have a lot of power and you'll be able to manipulate men easily."

She rubbed her arms, looking at the floor.

I gritted my teeth. Was she remembering the idiot who touched her?

"Can we turn it off?" she asked, her voice small.

I closed my eyes. "No, it's already starting."

"I don't want it." She stepped back from me, a frown creasing her forehead. "Is it true that a succubus will starve if she doesn't feed on men?"

"Eventually, yes."

Amma's lips thinned and she turned for the corridor. "I need to think."

I rubbed my neck, hating that I'd thrown all this at her, knowing the weight of it would crush that youthful happiness she had imagining a life, a boyfriend who loved her. But maybe knowing what her powers meant would keep her in her room a year or two longer, protected.

My stomach rumbled, telling me I'd left it too long since my last feed, but I wasn't leaving Amma now. I'd sleep off the hunger and find someone tomorrow.

Despite the hunger pangs, sleep came easily, but my dreams set my nerves alight.

A tanned man sitting on a log in the woods held an icon identical to mine. He turned its body over and over. His expression was set, so stern, as if he was working on a plan. And my succubus side wanted me to run my hands through the buzzed hair around his ears and tug on his longer hair, baring my neck to the nip of his wicked teeth.

But my heart was thumping through my ears with fear as well. He shouldn't have my icon. With that, he could control me like a puppet.

I stared past his long lashes, into his sexy eyes, and wondered what he was planning and what it meant for me. And then he looked at me, his eyes widening, and I woke up in bed, gasping for breath and swinging around. He wasn't here. My hand dove for my icon, and I gripped its comforting warmth. The coarse wood dug into my skin, but I didn't care. It was safe. I was safe.

2

Jaxon

Trees whipped past me, so fast the leaves would be a blur to human eyes. I snorted. Humans would have long ago fallen down the steep mountainside to my left in the dim twilight. Unlike them, I saw everything. Every breath, rush of wind, and bead of sweat was magnified. Not as much as in my wolf form, but enough that my evening patrol run brought a thrilling energy. I was one with my territory—with the woods, the air, and the moon.

My family had walked this territory for generations. Our grandfather had told my brother and me stories about the magic the mountain guarded. It was our special charge to care for it and make sure it never fell into the wrong hands.

Then my brother had become those wrong hands. I grimaced, leaping over a tangle of roots.

Twins have a special kind of bond, but as wolves and twin alphas, Zeke and I had been at each other's throats since we were infants. When I'd been chosen pack leader, Zeke could not handle it. He'd fought me every step of the way. I paused, sniffing the air. There was something different here.

Why was I wasting my time thinking about Zeke? He'd lost the pack fight, and he'd refused to submit to me. I'd generously given him and his new "pack" land at the base of the mountain, but he was still a thorn in my side.

I should have killed him. But he was my brother, my twin, and despite everything, it would be like murdering a part of myself.

I whipped uphill, on the homeward stretch, when a change of wind brought a musky smell to my nose. That's what I'd scented before and why I'd been thinking about Zeke.

Wolves, and not pack. I snarled. They had Zeke's stench all over them. I was not having his wolves sniffing around my territory. Or escaping before I taught them to observe the correct boundaries.

If he was going to lead a separate pack, then he needed to abide by the rules governing packs. One of the most basic was that wolves were required to give notice before entering another pack's territory.

I scowled. Bad enough I'd let them leave with my brother. Bad enough I hadn't forced them to submit. I couldn't let them get away with this. I couldn't have my pack thinking I was weak when it came to my brother.

Chucking off my clothes, I took a long whiff, my nose already turning into my wolf. Now I smelt maple, oak, pine, and the musty, salty, boozy taste of a wolf who had likely ventured into Tup's bar. I fell to my knees, grimacing against the change. The pain of the transformation had diminished with time and familiarity, but it was never comfortable. My fur rolled over me, replacing my skin.

Turning downhill, I raced for town. What idiot would invade another pack's territory for a couple of drinks?

Correction: two idiots. My wolf tracked them on their swaying path to their pickup truck. I was careful to keep upwind, but it hardly mattered. They hung off each other. How they thought they could drive in that state . . . I growled. *Their alpha should have them on a tighter leash.*

One unlocked the vehicle and reached for the door. I pounced, knocking him into the side of the truck. He fell limp, smacking his head against the rubber wheel. I sniffed him, but he wasn't known to me. Zeke must have been recruiting.

I turned and toppled the second, following him to the dusty ground. I snarled, baring my teeth, my saliva dripping onto his nose, but his chest rumbled with laughter.

The fool was laughing at me.

My wolf cocked its head, letting my human mind work it out. Inwardly, I cursed. The idiot who thought he could drink in my territory without begging for permission was my ex-pack mate—Cooper. And the other out-cold idiot must be the latest wolf he'd persuaded to go on a drinking rampage, scouting for women who didn't yet know their "love 'em and leave 'em" style.

I dug my claws into Cooper's chest, my wolf relishing his hiss and swearing complaint about my inability to lighten up. *So be it. A good alpha doesn't have the liberty of fun.*

"Are you going to tear my throat out—or stare me down with wolf eyes all night? You can't blame a man for missing Tup's," Cooper grouched, pushing onto his hands. "You know his BBQ ribs are all my dreams come true."

I jumped off him and shifted back into my human form. The breeze was too cold to be comfortable against my bare skin. But it added to my sharp, icy anger.

Situated on the end of Main Street—well, really the only street—in the tiny town of Hawkins, Tup's Bar and Grill did the best marinades and BBQ I'd ever tasted. Still, I wasn't about to admit I had one of his steaks waiting for me in the fridge and let Cooper get away with this behavior. Ex-pack mate or not, there were rules, and he'd left me.

I crossed my arms and stared, waiting for at least an attempt at contrition.

As usual, Cooper would sooner give up drinking than admit his mistakes. Though at least he dropped his gaze, deferring to my position.

Lunging down, I grabbed his ear and hauled him to his feet. A quick glance told me his buddy was still out cold by the passenger door.

"Keys?"

Cooper signaled to his pocket.

I took the keys and slung him in the cab of the truck. Then I threw his friend in with him.

My phone was with my discarded clothes, so I wouldn't get the chance to warn Zeke of the arrival of his clearly lost wolves. Not that he deserved a warning.

I rummaged in the back of the pickup for a spare set of clothes. Shifters always carried a couple. Cooper's shirt would be too tight around my shoulders, but the jeans would cover my ass for the drive.

Slipping into the driver's seat, I adjusted the mirrors, then looked over at my new charges. With the smell that came off of them, I should have thrown them in the back. Cooper had leaned against the window and promptly fallen asleep. A good decision on his part. Listening to his excuses and jokes the whole thirty-minute ride to their new pack would only make me angrier. That boy didn't even try to grow up.

The truck spluttered to life and I floored it, the wheels spinning and dirt flying as I rejoined the muddy side road. Trees flew by as I wound through the mountains and down to the other side, almost all the way to the city.

Our little community was tucked back into the mountains, but it didn't mean we didn't see our share of tourists. They mostly stayed in town at the bed and breakfast, eating at Tup's and hiking the hills. I'd instructed my wolves to avoid them. I could only hope my brother did the same. The last thing we needed was a confrontation between tourists and wolves—Cooper's drinking buddy slid toward me as I took the turn—even drunk ones. I wrinkled my nose and shoved him back onto his pack mate.

A few minutes later, I shut off the truck on the side of a minor road without lights which was lined by the last of the forest. A decent-sized territory and more than Zeke deserved. The city wasn't far, either. Plenty of drinking places there for his wolves to get into trouble.

I'd barely moved to switch off the headlights when two men walked out of the woods. One had curly hair and a beard and looked like he pumped iron for fun. The other was another one of my ex-pack mates, Vince.

Vince nodded to me and jerked his head at the truck cab. "Cooper and Dale inside?"

"If Dale is the other wolf that entered my territory uninvited, yes." I studied Vince. I always wondered what made the wolves choose Zeke over me. We'd all played together as pups. I knew this man almost as well as I knew myself. At least, I'd always thought I did.

The stranger shoved Cooper and his friend awake and dragged them out the truck.

I ignored their huffs and moans. I didn't care how drunk they were. They had to answer for this. "Take me to Zeke, Vince."

Vince's partner blew out his breath in a whistle. I snarled. I wasn't in the mood to go over how much trouble their pack mates were in, so I shoved past Vince, stalking toward the center of the woods.

He quickly flanked me, then moved one step ahead to lead the way. He shushed his partner too, knowing I was in no mood for chitchat.

A good fifteen minutes into the trees, I caught the flickering light of a fire and spotted Zeke, sprawled across a log, a bottle of bourbon in hand. That's my twin brother—setting such an excellent example.

"Jaxon, so good to see you." He opened his arms in mock greeting.

"I wish I could agree, Brother."

I shook my head at the state of him. As identical twins, looking at him was like seeing what I'd look like if I let myself follow every whim and instinct. What I'd look like if I had no sense. The very thought of getting into such a state where I was swaying on a log in front of my wolves made my stomach clench and squirm.

Zeke planted his bottle in the dirt, rising to face me.

Good. At least he was still able to stand.

"What are you doing here? I didn't give you an invite." His dark eyes flashed in the firelight, and his fingers twitched at his sides. "You can't barge in here whenever you feel like it."

I closed my eyes, hating that my nose flared with my deep breath. I preferred not to show how much this evening clawed at me. But Zeke had to get his pack in order. Especially Cooper. He'd had it tough when his mother left, and then his older brother had babied him, but having a wolf with the power to be alpha run around like a pup was embarrassing.

Jerking my thumb behind me to Cooper and his friend still struggling to stay upright, I said, "I found these two on my pack's property. I've delivered them to you. I assume they will be appropriately punished for trespassing?" I raised an eyebrow.

Zeke spat out his laughter. "Punished? For what? Visiting Tup's?"

I gritted my teeth. If Zeke let every small flaunting of his authority go, he'd quickly be challenged for control of his new pack, whether they were his friends or not. This was exactly why he couldn't be trusted as alpha.

"For invading another pack's land without permission or warning. You're lucky I brought them back unharmed. I was within my rights to drive them off." Or kill them, but that'd be my last resort with Cooper. He was a fool, but he was a fool I'd grown up with. Even if he did choose Zeke over me.

"What would you suggest I do, Brother?" Zeke leaned back, crossing his arms over his chest.

I wanted to slap that smirk off his face, but I forced myself to be calm, settling for shifting my stance and scowling. "That is your decision. It's your pack. Let me know what you decide." I turned to go.

"Hold on," Zeke said. "Vince will escort you back to your pack, with my thanks. Next time, warn me you're coming."

"Don't let there be a next time, Zeke, or I can't promise your wolves will come back unharmed."

A low growl spread through the wolves listening in, rumbling through the air like thunder. I ignored it and strode back through the woods toward the truck. Vince followed a few paces behind, not daring to break the silence.

3

Cooper

My cracking hangover kept me in the shadows of the woods around the campfire. I'd only had one or two sips of the bottle of bourbon that sat between my boots. Hair of the dog wasn't working for me. Jaxon dragging me back to camp and telling on me to Zeke hadn't helped my mood either. I rubbed my head. The throbs still stung, but they'd settle soon enough.

I was more worried about the jittery feeling in the air. Something was going down tonight. I could feel the wrongness of it—whatever it was—prickling along my skin. My wolf was demanding I stay right here, ready to protect our pack, and I agreed. That's why I wasn't scrolling through my phone, forgetting all my problems with a little no-strings-attached fun. I smiled, remembering the new waitress at Tup's. Candy, I think she'd said her name was. Long red locks that fell down her back and legs for days. I'd twisted my hands in it as I . . . the hair on my arms stood on end. Something was wrong.

I scanned the wolves around the fire and saw Zeke tap Vince's shoulder. He got up, and they moved deeper into the woods together.

Fuck. I gritted my teeth, my stomach bubbling with last night's liquor. The scruffy, scarred enforcer was useful, but he wasn't Zeke's number two. *I am.*

There was only one reason he'd have taken him instead of me. He was meeting that damned sorcerer. I'd made my feelings about that asshole plain, so Zeke had left me out—either as punishment or to avoid the fallout. That wasn't going to fly. I growled.

Pushing to my feet, I left my bourbon and wound through the trees after them.

Zeke and Vince were almost all the way back to the road by the time they stopped. Gabriel's tall, bony figure waited. Even in the near complete darkness, I made out his tailored suit and his dark hair cut short against his head.

I edged around the trees until I could see everyone's faces.

Gaunt with beady eyes and a slick smile, the sorcerer made my wolf bristle, ready to pounce. Everything about him felt off. His presence in our forest, on our mountain, was wrong. I didn't know why Zeke couldn't see it. Gabriel wasn't pack. And he couldn't be trusted. Hell, even Jaxon was more pack than this asshole.

Zeke was straight-faced and sober. That meant he didn't completely trust the sorcerer either. Maybe there was hope that I could talk him out of this deal.

My alpha's shadowed eyes cut into his visitor. "Gabriel, thank you for meeting me."

"Of course." The sorcerer dipped his chin. His eyes gleamed, greedy and eager. "Have you considered my offer?"

I barely held my snarl back. His offer wasn't worth listening to. I could understand Zeke being pissed he'd lost the alpha battle to Jaxon, but getting into bed with this nutso wouldn't help anything.

"I have," Zeke said.

Fuck no. Days after Zeke found that stupid wooden sculpture in his latest magical artifact haul, Gabriel turned up. He'd been a distant figure in our lives for months, helping Zeke track and identify artifacts.

Zeke had been obsessed with these lost objects since we were pups, always digging up the land searching for treasure. As he'd grown, he'd started searching farther afield, claiming he could feel the magic in these trinkets. But he'd never been able to make any of them work, at least not magically. Gabriel claimed he could.

And what's more, now Gabriel was offering to displace Jaxon in exchange for the chance to study the magic in our mountain. Too damned convenient if you asked me. Not that anyone had.

This was no passing visit either. Candy had given me an earful last night before my drink kicked in about the new developer in town and all his amazing plans for Hawkins. How he was going to make something of our mountain. Gabriel had told the humans he was looking to buy land. *Yeah, our land.*

I curled my hands into fists, glaring at the sorcerer's straight, confident posture. I didn't trust him. He had the voice of a salesman—all persuasive charm. He wouldn't take no for an answer. And Zeke ate up his wild stories of magic and power.

"What did you decide?" Gabriel asked.

"You're sure this demon can remove my brother from power?" Zeke asked, his brow wrinkling. "Without bloodshed?"

Demon? Now they were talking about calling up demons? That was dark and dangerous magic if it was true.

"Yes." Slime dripped from Gabriel's voice. What crypt had this guy come from? "This kind of demon is hypnotizing. She'll sway your brother to your will."

Zeke hunched his shoulders. His wolf could feel how wrong this was, and he was pushing through anyway. "And this demon—she'll be under my control?"

"With the icon, she'll be completely under control."

I couldn't take it anymore. How could Zeke believe this asshole was on our side? Jaxon had always said his brother lacked common sense, but I'd dismissed him. Jaxon controlled with an iron fist and demanded unblinking loyalty. To him, anything that wasn't his way was wrong and voicing it was a challenge. Going to him would be a last resort.

Confronting Zeke now would do nothing but get me a bloody nose and pour gasoline on his fire, but I couldn't let this go on. Pushing past the bushes, I strode out to where they could see me. My eyes flicked between Zeke, Gabriel, and Vince, who at least out of all of them had the sense to look guilty.

"Be clear, Alpha," I growled. "He didn't say this thing would be under *your* control."

Zeke narrowed his eyes. "I didn't invite you to this meeting."

I could feel his displeasure rolling over me, but I barreled on. He needed to hear this, and if not from me then who? "Zeke, you can't trust him. Don't take this deal. Please."

"You were restricted to camp," he muttered.

Fury snaked its way up my spine. I'd been his friend as well as his second. I'd chosen to leave the pack we'd grown up with *for him*, and he was treating me like an errant child. I snarled, "I'm not a damn pup. I'm your second." And I was trying to help him.

Running a hand through his short brown hair, Zeke sighed. "Not if you don't grow up and quit causing unnecessary trouble."

Like my alpha hadn't led the charge into almost every scrap of trouble I'd ever gotten into. Like he wouldn't have been drinking right alongside me at Tup's last night if he hadn't been off chasing artifacts. Zeke almost sounded like his brother. I snorted. He'd pound me senseless if I ever said that aloud.

Instead, I lifted my palms innocently and said, "I haven't left the woods." I smirked.

Zeke scowled.

Now that, I could never get away with in Jaxon's pack.

My gaze fell to the wooden sculpture Zeke turned over in his hands. I'd never thought this tiny thing, of all the strange artifacts he'd acquired over the years, would be the one which started something.

I had to talk him through this, show him how insane using it was.

Pointing to the figure, I asked, "Aren't these things supposed to be powerful?"

Zeke nodded.

"And controlling this demon—their power—will help us take back the mountain?" Our families had all lived on the mountain his brother ruled—that Zeke wanted to rule—for generations. We'd always known the mountain had deep magic that we could barely touch, *and* we knew we needed to protect it from outsiders. *Like Gabriel.* And here Zeke was trying to give it away. He wasn't seeing things straight.

"Get to the point, Cooper," Zeke muttered.

The irritation in his tone had my wolf bristling, calling for me to challenge him. But I didn't want to fight for head of the pack. I'd never wanted that. If I'd desired to be alpha, I'd have gone with my older brother to find new wolves to rule. Billy still kept in touch, telling me all the joys of being under his own rule. And even though my brother had raised me when Dad died and Mum ran off, I'd stayed here. The mountain was my home and Zeke was more than my alpha. He was a brother to me, too.

I just didn't want him to do something stupid.

A light wind curled around me, barely a whisper of the land's power here on what used to be the very edges of our pack's property, the back end of nowhere Jaxon had 'gifted' us when Zeke lost the alpha fight and left Jaxon's pack.

I watched Zeke's face. He knew this was wrong, but I couldn't count the number of things Zeke and I had done together that we both knew were terrible ideas. That wouldn't stop him. *Think, Cooper. There must be some way to talk my alpha out of this.*

"Why give an outsider control?" I jerked my thumb at Gabriel. "It goes against everything you've worked for. You took those artifacts to *stop* people like him from using them."

Studying Zeke's face, I grimaced. He hadn't even blinked. He'd always felt less—less important, less powerful, less alpha—than Jaxon. Taking back the mountain with an artifact Jaxon had dismissed as harmless would seem like the ultimate coup—but it risked our pack, our lives, even the mountain.

I moved between Zeke and the sorcerer, cutting off his view, and clasped my alpha's arms. I spoke low, so the sorcerer wouldn't hear. "I know Jaxon's never treated you right, but this isn't the way to set things straight."

Hell, I probably hadn't helped, getting dragged back here last night, proving once again that his brother had the upper hand and the best bar around. But if Zeke did this, the two of them would never make amends. And they'd never reunite the pack. My gut twisted. More than anything, I wanted peace between what had been my two best friends. But using this sorcerer would mean war.

Zeke snarled at me, and I dropped my hands.

"Your objection is noted, Cooper," he said, bitterness coating his words.

I bowed my head, showing submission. I'd embarrassed Zeke, and he'd make me pay for it. He had to. I was an alpha in my own right and maybe could have fought for the pack. Giving in to me endangered his position. But he had to know I only wanted to protect him.

He stepped to the side and looked beyond me to the sorcerer. "We have a deal."

I closed my eyes and blew out my breath, then looked to Vince. He tried to hide it, but I saw the stiffness in his stance, the twitch to his hands. He was as worried as me.

4

Del

My ex's crappy door shook under the weight of my beating fist, but he wasn't answering. After days of those two identical men and a third sexy looker-on plaguing my dreams, I was done waiting to find out what was going on. Especially since I couldn't seem to feed on anyone since the dreams started. All I could think about was those three damned hot, devilish men.

This shit was exactly the kind of thing Prax would do to me, hoping he'd make my hunger cramps bad enough that I'd return to him and plead for his help. He'd bank on me being so scared over my icon I'd run to him. I wouldn't be surprised if he'd hired the "seer". It was too convenient Prax just happened to turn up at my party that night.

Ugh. Screw this. I slammed my boot against the door, rattling the wood in the frame. And again.

Snap. The door gave way.

"Asshole! What did you do this time?" My gaze scoured the room for him. He wasn't lounging in the dump of a living room, which was littered with bright lacy panties of various sizes. Explained why he didn't answer the door. He'd be basking in the afterglow and considering another round, and stuff the consequences.

I stormed into his bedroom.

Three women curled around my ex in a heap of flesh and limbs. I crossed my arms and tapped my foot.

Prax smiled up at me from the middle of the bundle, like a cat with more cream than he knew what to do with. "Come to join us, Del?"

The smell of his room was salt, sweat, and a binding vine of lust that wrapped around my arm. Mentally, I tore through it. "Never again."

His eyes slid over me, a hint of hunger in their depths. "We were good together—you and I."

I shook my head. "We were suckers attracted to our own compulsion."

He slipped from the bed, wrapping a sheet around his waist out of respect for me. He knew that I hated unnecessary displays. Especially when my body still responded to him as if we'd never broken up. He crossed to the bureau and poured a glass of dark red wine.

I squeezed my hands into fists, resisting the need to crawl into bed with him. I hadn't eaten last night, and now my hunger was unabated.

Taking a sip of his drink, Prax watched me. "We are capable of love, you know," he said. "Even demons like you and me."

Bullshit, I muttered mentally. "That's not why I'm here."

He sighed and leaned his elbow on the dresser. "Then to what do I owe this visit?"

"Have you been messing with my dreams?"

Convincing me someone had my icon was exactly the kind of mind game that'd please him after I dumped his ass. Normal men took rejection hard. An incubus took it as a slight against his powers. He hadn't stopped trying to win me back or snub me since.

"You know I don't have that ability."

I scoffed. He had plenty of women at his disposal to do the legwork for him. "That doesn't answer my question."

"Tell the truth, I've barely thought of you since your last party." He studied me, like he thought that'd scrape my emotions.

And it did, but not in the way he wanted. Cold, stabbing fear weighed me down. Prax wasn't smirking, trying to hide his glee. That sucked-in impish face was his go-to, and I wasn't seeing it. Which meant he didn't do this. And if these dreams weren't down to Prax, then what was causing them? Were they a warning?

I'd try one last time. "Did you alter my dreams and have men take my icon?"

Prax frowned. "It's not at the end of your necklace?" He pointed to the cord around my neck.

"That one is."

Demons with parents from two species had two icons. If that was the case for me, I might not be as safe as I thought. My research said the two icons were identical, the shape representing the demon's soul rather than their species. And the icon in my dreams was a perfect copy of mine.

His eyes widened. "You have two?" The shock in his voice was far too clear, and the bastard couldn't act to save his life.

I gritted my teeth. "Do you know anything, anything at all, about where a second icon might be?"

Slowly, he shook his head. "I thought you were all succubus." He tilted his head. "Perhaps that's why you so intrigued me."

I threw my hands up and turned on my heel. No point staying if the cretin had no idea why I was dreaming about a man holding an icon that tugged at my soul.

My breath came a little faster when the hot outside air hit me, but I shoved down the panic. Tarzi would know what was going on. I rubbed my eyes so hard I saw stars, then singled out a portal maker in the passing lunch rush. I grabbed his arm and used my charm to persuade him to give me transport.

He was a short demon with spiky horns along his bald head. Turning, he lay his orange hoop on the ground, marking the spot for the portal.

"Where are you wanting to go?" he asked, his squeaky voice grating against my nerves.

It wasn't his fault I was freaking out. The underling demon was just trying to do his job. I bit back my bark of ire and gave him the address as sweetly as I could. I was cheating him out of his coin already, but I had left the house in too much of a hurry and hadn't brought any.

He murmured an archaic chant over the ring. Portal demons didn't need to say anything to make a gate, but it made travelers feel better if it looked like he was working hard for his payment. Since I hadn't paid him, he didn't need to do it at all. But still, habits are hard to break.

Within moments, green smoke clouded the ring. The demon turned to me, a grin stretched across his round face. "At your pleasure, madam."

I nodded and stepped into the circle. Every travel experience was different. Sometimes I felt like my insides were becoming outsides. Sometimes a great force pushed on me from above, making me feel as squat as the portal demon. This time, a tickle of leaves ran over my skin and I exhaled. Not a bad journey then.

Minutes later, I stood outside my best friend's house. A small building, more cottage than house. Thorny climbers curved around the windows and swung from the thatched roof. Behind it, sentient trees clustered, whispering among themselves.

"Yes, it's me again," I muttered at them, and they bowed toward me. My friend preferred the quiet and peace of nature to the crowded colonies of demons. I couldn't say I blamed her, having moved out of the succubus neighborhood as soon as I could.

I lingered on the step and bit my lip.

Tarzi dealt in dreams and fed off nightmares. She'd know what was really happening here. But despite the dread every time I saw that man touch my icon, I almost didn't want to let the dreams go.

Every time I closed my eyes, I saw the three men. They seemed so alive, like I could reach out and feel their skin beneath my palms. I was used to beauty—there was plenty of that to go around in Hell—but there was something about these men that was different, that affected me strangely.

One was a strong man with a hard jaw, stubble, hair buzzed short on the sides and longer on top, and the most commanding golden hazel eyes. He stared through me as he stood on the edge of a mountain, within the clouds, surveying his domain. His muscles rippled with power and authority. An alpha male, through and through.

And the same man, but different. This time deep within a forest, the flickering campfire showing the amber tones to his bourbon and highlighting how his eyes flashed with easy humor. And naughtiness, like he'd pull me between the sheets and tease and pleasure me until I couldn't move or speak from an overdose of sensation. I licked my lips. He'd tickle my darkest desires. And imagining the two of them, their smooth, tattooed and tanned skin, was more than enough to shoot my appetite into the stars.

But another man lingered in the shadows of that campfire, leaning back against a tree. He drew my attention the most. His loud laughter and quiet, watchful presence in a conversation. A good listener. Kind eyes and a slow sexy smile, his lower lip tucked between his teeth. He knew exactly what he did to a woman. His laidback attitude and the warm, coppery brown skin beneath his buzzed black hair. His clothes were simple—low slung jeans and a casual shirt, but he knew how to wear them . . . he was gorgeous. He was also the personality I most recognized. A player. The male version of me, in a way.

The three of them together had me on edge, and not just because one had an icon. They were so attractive, they filled my mind and made it hard to feed on other men. The others didn't compare.

The door opened and I jumped.

Tarzi looked at me and shook her head. "You've been standing here for five minutes, licking your lips and swaying like you might fall over.

Were you ever going to open the door and say hello? Or were you waiting for me to realize you were here? There is a doorbell and a knocker, and you know where they are because you've used them every other visit."

I ducked my head. "Sorry. It's . . . well. It's why I came."

She shooed me into the cozy living room. Tarzi always knew just how to decorate. The good and bad side of her powers were equally unsettling and made her crave physical, touchable comfort around herself.

I sat on her low, puffy couch, which always seemed to eat me whole. I battled the cushions but quickly gave up. I always lost that fight, and Tarzi's eyes weren't losing any of their piercing accusations.

She crossed her arms. "You should've come to me days ago." She looked me over again, her lips thinning. "I've not seen you this hungry since you left your mother's place."

Her worry and judgment singed the air between us, but she was right. I shouldn't have left it this long before seeing her. Dreams were her area. But seeing my men—those men—felt so personal. I hadn't wanted to share.

I blew out my breath and swallowed against my dry throat, trying not to think about how much my hands itched to twist together. Telling her didn't feel right, but it was my best way forward.

"I've been having some strange dreams. Repeating dreams." I nibbled on my lip. "Can you tell me if anyone is manipulating them?"

She'd wrapped a long gauzy shawl around her narrow shoulders. The greens and browns of it were grounding, reflecting the nature around her home. With her chestnut hair loose over her shoulders and her thin frame, Tarzi looked as though she'd be knocked over by a strong wind. But I knew my friend had an iron spine. She'd been my rock over the years. I could always count on Tarzi to be honest with me.

She gazed at me, considering.

"Prax said he didn't do it," I said with a shrug, "but we both know he rarely tells the truth."

31

And there were other options. That seer being one. Maybe he wanted me to pay him for more information? Using dreams for a scam was a creative tactic. The right partnership could rake in a lot of coin.

Tarzi leaned closer and took my hands in hers, smoothing the back of my palms. For a moment, I thought this might be part of her process, but her eyes were too soft.

"Del, honey, you really should've come to me. Beating yourself up over this and investigating every angle, and including your ex, isn't the best way to find answers here."

I made a non-committal noise. Those methods usually worked.

But Tarzi had already closed her eyes. They moved under her eyelids, like she was searching through my mind. Perhaps she was. Or perhaps she looked at the edges of it for tethers or links or manipulation. I had no idea how her mare powers worked. She fed off nightmares like I fed off people. I hadn't wanted or needed to know anymore until now.

Her eyes fluttered open, and she placed my hands back on my lap before withdrawing into her seat. She licked her lips, shaking her head slightly. "I didn't see anything." Her brow furrowed. "You say these dreams have repeated? How many times, and what happened in them?" Again, her eyes were crystal clear as they stared into mine. She knew I was hiding something.

"I see three men. Deliciously gorgeous men." I smiled, and she grinned back.

"Is that why you haven't been eating right? You have a craving?"

"Yeah. All three are . . . sexy." I shook my head. They were more than that. Something about them held my attention like nothing else, but I couldn't explain it.

She rolled her eyes. "Well, don't get too picky. They're probably not real."

I sucked in my lip. "About that . . . a seer came to my last party."

"Is that who you last indulged in?"

Her tone was curious, but I could feel the worry rolling off her. Did I look that bad? I grimaced and said, "No. But he predicted my icon would be stolen. Said he saw me in chains."

She looked at my chest. "But your icon . . ."

I tapped the icon through my top. "It's still here. But these men in my dreams were holding another icon. It looked identical, and it tugged at me."

Tarzi nibbled on her lip. "If it's not your succubus icon, if you think you might have a second icon . . ." Her eyes softened. "You know who you have to talk to."

I rubbed my face. "I was really hoping you wouldn't say that." I looked at her again. "You're absolutely sure there's no manipulation of my dreams? This is either my imagination or it's real?"

"Sorry, Del. I wish I had better news." She rubbed her hands against her thighs, her fingers twitching. "If you need any help finding this icon and these men, you will ask me?"

"Of course." My stomach was writhing like snakes. I needed to feed, but seeing my mother put me off the idea far more than my dreams. I stood. "If I have to see her, I should get going."

Tarzi inclined her head. "Keep me updated?"

I pulled her into a hug and smiled against her shoulder. "Thank you for your help."

5

Cooper

It was late—or early, depending on how you looked at it. I had the late-night watch, and the energy in the camp was off again, bristling with electricity, humming through my feet. It was growing more intense, overpowering the natural breeze and the flow of magic from the mountain. Someone was working magic; I was sure of it. My nose twitched, my wolf itching to run after that sorcerer and stomp his magic out, like a smoldering forest fire.

I looked around for Zeke. He'd know exactly what this was.

There. Striding toward me from his RV. His eyes were full of fire, pinning me to the spot. Yeah, no chance Zeke was letting me interrupt whatever ritual he'd set up with the sorcerer when he was in that mood. I'd be lucky if he'd let me speak at all.

And pressing him now, less than a week after my last attempt . . . well, that could get me thrown out of the pack. I'd already pushed him further than I should have.

Zeke grabbed my arm and yanked me away from the campfire, back into the tree line. I didn't resist. If he wanted to ream me out, best he do it in private.

He kept walking until the other wolves' voices were barely a whisper and Gabriel's fiery magic was more tickle than burn. It cleared my head and calmed my mood. Perhaps it did the same for Zeke because he looked more like himself, more relaxed, than he had in weeks.

He dropped my arm. "I need you to do something for me."

I rubbed my chin. Last time we'd talked, he'd insisted he knew what was right for the pack. Then he'd told me to keep my nose out of the sorcerer business. So this must be something else.

"Has something happened?" I asked. "Do we have a new wolf? Or does someone need to be punished?"

"No, nothing like that."

I tapped my fingers against the rough bark of a nearby tree, my mind spinning with what this could be about. I glanced at Zeke. "Then what?" My voice came out harsher than I intended.

Zeke's shoulders hunched slightly.

I was being too aggressive. I needed to tread softly, use the good old Cooper charm for something useful this time.

Zeke sighed. "I need you at the ritual. After Gabriel has done his bit with the icon, wait until he's looking the other way and then take it. Keep hold of it for me until the spell is over. I'm sure that's the key to controlling the demon, and I can't risk him taking command of it. If this demon is strong enough to sway Jaxon, they're strong enough to sway me."

Thank hell he'd listened to part of what I'd said. And he still trusted me. My ears were ringing, and inside, my wolf was howling with unbounded glee, but, with difficulty, I kept my face blank. "You're sure about this? You want me to help, not Vince?" Okay, screw it, the bitterness seeped in there.

The corner of Zeke's mouth quirked up. "Yes, you're my second." He rolled a shoulder. "And Gabriel is used to seeing Vince. He won't question it if you're missing."

I frowned then. Was this planned? Or was that wishful thinking? In the end, it didn't matter. I let my held breath go. "When are we doing this?"

"In about thirty minutes. You'll follow us out there, at a distance."

That explained the ramping tension in the air, burning through the usual calming breeze of the mountain's magic. They were almost ready.

"How do I know when he's finished with the icon part of the ritual?" I asked.

"He talked me through it," Zeke said with a grimace.

I took that as a hopeful sign that he didn't like this foul magic any more than I did.

He continued, "Gabriel has to channel the icon to summon the demon. He'll coat the figure in blood and bury it in the earth at some important spot."

"I dig it up once he's done that part?" I scratched the back of my neck. It could work. If the artifact was the key.

"Exactly." Zeke ran his hand through his hair. "I'll draw him away long enough for you to duck in."

"Got it." I could do that. Though I still didn't like the idea of calling this demon or its power to our land. Too much about the whole process was unknown.

Zeke clasped my arm. "Be ready," he said, meeting my eyes. Then he marched back to camp.

I followed him at a much slower pace. I was glad Zeke wasn't completely taken in by this nutso, but going through with the spell . . . it was so risky. And if Zeke maintained control of the icon, providing that *was* the part of all this that controlled the demon . . . he could still move ahead against Jaxon. With an actual demon.

My wolf whimpered in my mind in sympathy. If we did what Zeke asked, we'd be helping him topple Jaxon. He'd have no idea what was coming for him, and who knew what this demon would do to dethrone him. And Zeke . . . I couldn't tell anymore how far he'd go to get his way.

Would he hurt his brother, his brother's pack? I knew he hated control, but a demon was a massive wildcard. We'd never done anything with so much potential to blow our faces off.

I pinched the bridge of my nose and searched out a long gulp of bourbon back in camp. Even with the spirit slipping down my throat, I couldn't relax. Gabriel's magic was a constant irritant. I scratched an itch and frowned. A strange rash circled my wrists and inner elbows, like a heat rash. A side effect of the dark magic in the air? I rubbed my hands together, trying to claw back a moment of peace, of space to think.

I had no good choices . . . If I went against Zeke, I could lose my place here. Jaxon was so high strung, he'd never take me back unless I groveled. Which wasn't happening. But my wolf and I were sure Zeke's plan would end in disaster.

Ugh, losing myself in women was so much easier than politics.

A while later, Zeke met my eyes across the campfire and minutely dipped his chin. It was time.

Zeke and Vince slipped into the trees.

I waited another minute or two, listening to the crackle of wood in the fire, watching the dance of the flames. I knew what I had to do.

I stood and followed them. Or rather, I followed the burn of magic, cringing against it as I got closer and closer to the mountain. They'd moved quickly and far to the south of our territory. By the time they stopped, we were just over the border into Jaxon's part of the woods, marked by his pack's mountain symbol on alternating tree trunks. I bit my tongue and walked through the dividing line, into his territory. No going back now.

Zeke, Vince, and Gabriel huddled around a large stone boulder. The sorcerer was using an indent in the rock as a kind of altar. He'd already slit his hand and was dripping his blood onto the icon. Then he passed a second knife to Zeke, who did the same. That's when Gabriel started mumbling. I wondered if it was all for show, but the air around me tightened, like it'd cinched into two points: the double circle of salt and flickering candles on the ground and the icon.

Each breath came hard and rough down my throat. How could Zeke and Vince stand to be so close to it? The magic was bitter and foul.

Carefully, Gabriel wiped his hands and took the icon in a roughly northern direction, where he buried it at the base of a very old tree. He swiped the back of his dirty hand across his face, scowling. Then he stood and turned back to the circle. His eyes scanned the trees, looking for me, I supposed.

Zeke moved toward the sorcerer, but Gabriel was already returning to his altar, his back to the spot where he had buried the icon.

Perfect. My turn. I edged around the ritual and walked through the shadows until I was inches away from the disturbed dirt.

I glanced at Zeke, Vince, and Gabriel, but none of them were looking my way. *Good.* Lifting my hand, I let the change run over it, part-shifting to use my claws. My wolf howled within me, wanting to be free to run away from the wrongness of this ritual. But we had work to do first. I dug through the earth, pushing aside small rocks and roots. The sorcerer hadn't put it too deep. Why hadn't I found it yet?

I peered around at the others. Their eyes were on the altar. But as I burrowed, a plan formed in my mind. Zeke wasn't going to like it, but it might be the only way to end this war before it began. I sighed when my paw found the rough wood of the icon and I shifted my hand back to scoop it out of the hole.

The wood felt warm in my hands, and sticky from the blood and dirt. But how could it be warm after a dunking in the cool earth? Magic, I guess?

Shrugging off the weirdness, I shoved the artifact in my pocket and snuck away from the ritual until I put enough distance between me and them to sprint without being heard.

The icon felt like iron in my pocket, far heavier than it should be, and it was steadily getting hotter.

I glanced through the trees at the lights of the camp and curved around it for my truck. My mind was made up. I couldn't let this thing derail our pack.

First, I tried to break the icon with my wolf's strength. No luck. I tucked the three inches of solid wood under my truck's tire.

My heart beat erratically as I fished for the keys and started the engine, but the truck moved over the icon like a bump in the road. No audible cracks.

I checked the artifact. Not so much as a splinter had come off it.

I cursed, then threw it on the passenger seat and tore along the rough back roads up the mountain as the solid black of the night sky lightened to a deep blue.

Crossing the borderlines didn't feel dangerous anymore. It was necessary. And the ride up the mountain was over in no time.

I hadn't even pulled the truck to a complete stop when wolves slid out of the shadows, growling so loud they drowned out the engine. Shit, but it was going to be a bitch convincing Jaxon I wanted to help.

6

Del

My steps echoed in the lofty marble-floored corridor which led to my mother's apartment. She'd moved into one of the largest succubus communities after my sister and I finally got our own place away from her, and boy, did I hate to visit. The whole building was extravagant: rich with fabric wall hangings, gauzy curtains, and gold-leaf painted ceilings designed by the best artists. And none of that luxury disguised the throb of music and the muffled *oof oof* or the knocks and thumps through the doors that left any visitor in no doubt that this was succubus territory. Living here, I'd be confronted with what I was every waking minute.

Mentally bracing myself, I drew up beside apartment number thirty-one and rang the old-fashioned rope doorbell. Then I wiped my hands on my leather pants.

The rhythmic noises on the other side of the door didn't stop, so I continually rang the bell. When I still didn't get an answer, I pounded on the door, skipping knocking completely. Still nothing. With a snarl, I kicked at the wood, slamming it with my boot.

Finally, the sexual noises inside stopped, and footsteps approached. Someone unlocked the door.

It opened a crack, enough for me to see my mother's cat wing eyeliner and heavy make-up. She looked me over, smiled, and pulled the door all the way open.

I winced. "You could've covered up first."

"Why? You know what we are."

I shook my head. I may be used to sex, but I'd never wanted to see my mother naked, her blonde hair stuck to her shoulders with sweat. Some things shouldn't be shared.

Over her shoulder, five men watched her with complete, eyes-glazed-over adoration. One of them turned his eyes to me, suddenly hopeful. I cringed. *Not* going to happen. Internally, I marked these five as demons I would never touch. Mother's cast-off pile grew every month.

Mother ushered me inside and closed the door. "How can I help?"

And that was how most of our conversations went these days. All I heard was "what need can I fulfill as your mother before you go away again." I sighed. She was never the maternal, hand-holding type. Not that I'd know what to do with her if she was.

Again, I glanced over her shoulder to her men. My passive powers were well in the room now, and two were looking me over in a way that made my insides squirm. I felt dirty. Not because they weren't hot, but because my powers would happily cross the "sleep with the mother or the daughter but not both" boundary.

I shook my head. "I was hoping we could talk alone. Is there somewhere we can go?"

She'd never get rid of her entertainment and I wouldn't want to sit on that sofa anyway. As a rule, I tried to touch as little as possible in her apartment. I knew she liked to mark places sexually with her men. Or they did. She bent to their desires as often as she bent them to hers. If only I could have the same level of wanton enthusiasm, but no. I was saddled with a desire for men to want me for my personality. Hey, a girl can dream.

41

I frowned. Maybe if my father wasn't an incubus, that need was the other half of me shining through.

My mother motioned to the kitchen. I moved in ahead of her and walked to the far side of the room. The countertops were pristine white, and the window at the far end overlooked a quiet little courtyard. I exhaled.

"What's going on? Is it Amma?" she asked, the thoughtful look on her face mocking the barely passing interest she took in our lives. "Her powers must be kicking in about now."

I clenched my teeth. I knew what she was hinting at, and like hell I'd let her "train" Amma in the best way to use her powers. She'd grow up ordinary for as long as possible. "It's not about Amma."

Her eyebrow raised. "Then what? Are you having trouble with something?" Her lip quirked because she'd told me before we left that I couldn't hack it alone, that I'd need to be with my kind, in the community. But she didn't want us and she didn't care about our happiness. She just wanted to be right.

"It's about my icon."

Her lips flatlined. "You lost it?"

"No." I bit my tongue. Was it better to pull off the scab quick or slow? Faster could slice through her defenses better. "Who was my father?"

Her chin drew back, her eyes wide. "What makes you ask that?"

"Just answer the question. Who was he?"

"I told you before that I'm not sure. The truth is, you're the result of a particularly busy evening. Pinpointing exactly which man your father was, well . . ." She rolled a shoulder and smiled prettily in a way which would get her off the hook with any man. But not me.

Not that there was much point in pressing her on a name. I'd tried that for years. She never put the effort in to work out who my father was. She probably didn't even remember the men she was with that night. They were just food to her. But this time I could ask something else, something that might focus her memory. "What was he?"

She blinked, her long lashes fluttering. "An incubus. You know that. You've never shown any other powers."

"Then why am I getting dreams about a second icon and having a seer tell me someone wants to use it against me?"

She pursed her lips. "You're sure you haven't lost your icon?"

I pulled it out of my top by the cord. Something I was having to do a lot lately. For my reassurance as much as others'.

"These dreams could be imaginings. I can see you're hungry. Maybe you're bored and want to try something new. To be controlled, maybe. To have more dominant men. That's something many women enjoy. I can recommend—"

"No. No recommendations." I rubbed the back of my neck. It felt clammy, and the stale sweat in the air was turning sour. As much as my mother thought my father was an incubus, there was no way she could be sure. She slept with all kinds of demons. It was only a guess that I was all sex demon.

"Don't get so worried over this. I'm sure it's nothing."

Right. Because the wait-and-see approach was going to make me feel better. I crossed back through the apartment, eyes on the floor so I wouldn't have to look at her man buffet again. That'd stir up the fish like blood in the water. "I'm going now."

"That's all you wanted?" she asked, following me. She tried to sound sorry, but her tone came out hopeful, which was probably closer to the truth.

"Yes, get back to your orgy. Have a good time."

"Oh, thank you. I hope you find some suitable men tonight, too." Now she narrowed her eyes and nodded for good measure. "At least four. You really do look starved."

I left before she could make any more suggestions. My first stop had to be my place. Amma needed to know what to do and who to trust if by some chance my mother's wild guesses were wrong and this second icon pulled me under the control of these three men. I shuddered. Amma wasn't ready to make it alone. First thing in the morning, I'd talk to her.

7

Jaxon

I took my breakfast outside, watching the light creep across the sky. Early mornings in camp were quiet and peaceful. Coffee, made with milk and sugar, and a full plate of eggs and bacon was the perfect preparation for a day spent coaching a pup through their first transition and the only excitement I wanted so early.

I growled when an all-too-unwelcome blue pickup truck careened into camp. Dirt billowed behind it as it skidded to a stop. The door opened, and Cooper dropped to the ground, empty hands held up in surrender.

I gritted my teeth and winced when they squeaked. He didn't have the right to be here, ex-pack or not, and I didn't like thinking about what I was going to have to do. It'd been easy enough to haul him home to Zeke after Tup's, but here the eyes of my wolves were on me. Even at four or five in the morning, I was never really alone among the pack. I had to make an example of him.

"Why are you here?" I snarled, setting my plate aside and lunging to my feet.

"Don't worry," he said, a pleading look on his face. "I'm not here to flaunt your precious rules. I need to speak with you."

"But you are flaunting them." I curled my hands into fists as I marched closer.

My sentries erupted from the woods around us, surrounding Cooper. I frowned. Not the best response time if it had been a real attack. I'd deal with them later.

Cooper took something out of his front pocket. A piece of wood whittled into the shape of a curvy woman. It was covered in blood.

I grunted, waving my wolves back to patrol. Cooper was mine to punish, and whatever that dirty piece of junk was, it didn't require back up. I'd rather keep my wolves on patrol in case this strange story was a distraction to cover an attack.

"What is that? Another one of Zeke's collection items?"

Why the hell would Cooper bring that to me like he'd done a good deed? He wasn't a puppy to be patted on the head. Though he acted like it. Whatever his poor reasoning, he had broken the rules, and I'd warned him what the consequence was.

Cooper stiffened, all humor falling from his face. "This one is dangerous."

I stilled. I'd never seen any of Zeke's artifacts do anything, but there was something about the expression on Cooper's face that gave me pause. "Dangerous how? And why would that be my problem?"

Cooper waved his hand as if that didn't matter. "I don't know how much time we have, but we need to destroy it."

I raised an eyebrow. "And Zeke can't help you why?" I didn't want to hurt my old friend, even if it was required, so I let him stall me.

For a moment, Cooper ducked his head, but then he met my eyes again, full of renewed fire. "My alpha wants to keep it. But trust me, you want this icon gone before they complete their spell."

Spell? Zeke was doing a spell? "You're making this up."

Cooper sucked air in through his teeth, his hands turning to fists.

He was getting impatient. So what? I didn't owe him anything. I was almost one hundred percent sure he was wasting my time.

"This icon calls a demon. With a sorcerer's help, Zeke will use the demon to remove you from power."

I watched him closely, but I didn't see any sign of nerves. Just anger and worry. And Cooper had always played it straight with things that mattered. If not for that, I would've dismissed this straight away. The very idea of demons was mad, but there had been rumors about summonings before . . . not that many first-hand witnesses seemed to survive for long. All of the summonings had needed an object which held something of the demon. Their icon.

And if Cooper was coming here, risking his place in his pack, he must want to tap into the mountain's power. But was that to complete this spell or destroy this icon?

I crossed my arms. "Did you at least try to break it yourself?"

"I tried. If my truck and my wolf can't so much as splinter it . . ."

"Let me see," I muttered. I didn't want to admit my interest. Maybe looking at it would tell me what made it so durable.

Cooper placed the icon in my palm. Immediately, his whole body relaxed and mine tensed. The icon had a weight that it shouldn't, and it was warm, far warmer than the air temperature.

I stared into the icon's whittled face and tried to assess its power with my wolf's senses. His fur bristled, and he rumbled with a growl, pawing at the ground as if to pounce on the icon and use it as a chew toy. I blew out my breath. Not good. My wolf hadn't done that since Zeke challenged me for alpha.

I cocked my head, waiting a moment.

Yes, the mountain's calming winds, its peaceful magic, had receded away from this thing. I hadn't noticed until I reached out with my senses.

Whatever this was, it was dangerous. And I wasn't leaving it in Zeke's hands. Cooper was right to bring it to me. And I wouldn't have to kill him for trespassing.

"Follow me, Cooper."

I'd call on the mountain's magic to break this thing apart. The mountain's magic hadn't been invoked for such a purpose since my grandfather's time, but I knew all the stories. The concentration of pure magic at the peak of the mountain could vaporize any threat.

I took the lead, and Cooper followed in tense silence.

As we walked through the trees and up the almost vertical path, the icon grew heavier. Strange, since it wasn't any bigger. It still fit in the palm of my hand.

Frowning, I drew the icon closer to my body to compensate, but in a few minutes even that tired me. A damned piece of wood couldn't best a shifter. I called my wolf to the surface so that I felt the fur brushing the underside of my skin. Now, my fingers tingled with heat. How could wood grow hotter?

I bit my tongue, passing the item back and forth between my hands. We were halfway up the mountain, and the icon was burning my fingers like a pan fresh out the oven. Could I keep hold of it all the way to the top? I had to. My pack depended on me, and I knew from the deep uncomfortable churning of my gut that this artifact was dangerous. I needed to destroy it.

Cooper was looking the other way, so I switched hands again and glanced at my wounded palm. All my fingers and the palm were throbbing and red. I swallowed past my dry throat and judged how far we were from the peak. Another ten minutes at least, even at a full run. I considered shifting to wolf form, but I didn't want my mouth to be burnt like my hands.

I upped my pace and switched the icon between my hands a few more times, but the pain was searing now, like I'd touched a white-hot poker. I gritted my teeth and pressed ahead anyway, because something told me that the icon was ramping up to something.

Cooper wasn't looking away now. I couldn't switch hands. I broke into a fast walk, but the weight of the artifact slowed me. I wasn't going anywhere near my normal pace. This heat was burning faster than I could heal. How had the wood not combusted? *Would* the mountain destroy this?

"Jaxon, stop being an idiot."

I switched from my fast walk into a jog, pretending it was out of annoyance, but really, I had to get this thing out my hands. Fast. "Don't call me an idiot when I'm doing you a favor."

He grabbed my arm and uncurled my fingers, grabbing the icon for himself. I opened my mouth to protest but he was staring at my hand.

"Shit, Jaxon, you've lost skin. You know being a leader doesn't mean enduring pain for your pride, right?"

I grunted, but I was glad I could get a rest, allowing my werewolf genes to work on the second-degree burns. Much longer, and it would have burned through my flesh, into my muscle, and that might've needed a shift to fix.

Cooper looked to the peak of the mountain. "Maybe another mile." He stared me down. "We're sharing this from here on out, okay?"

Grudgingly, I nodded. As much as I hated to admit it, I couldn't carry it alone, and I doubted there was time to go back to base and pick up tongs or an oven mitt. If this thing was going nuclear, we had to destroy it soon.

For the next half a mile, we dropped all pretense of a leisurely jog. We ran as fast as our shifter bodies could move in human form, the icon flying between us like the game hot potato, hand to hand and person to person.

We made great progress, and I wished I'd relented earlier. We'd have been at the top by now. But—shit.

A wayward throw from Cooper dropped the icon on the ground, too far for even my reflexes to save the catch. I stopped and hurried after it as it rolled downhill, losing us precious miles.

But the icon soon stopped of its own accord, rocking back and forth like it was laughing at me.

I bent to pick it up.

Red and blue flames hissed up around the icon like a blowtorch, blasting hot air at my face.

Blinking rapidly, I reared back, the hot air agitating my already burnt palms.

Fire consumed the wood, hiding its details, but the icon didn't burn. Holding it like this would be like holding a glowing coal, so I stomped on the wood, trying to put it out.

I quickly stopped. "The damn thing burns through my damned shoes. We can't carry it up the mountain like this."

Cooper nodded, hesitating as if to move toward my pack's camp. "I could run and get something to hold it?"

"We don't have time."

Tentatively, I reached toward it, but within inches all I could sense was white-hot pain. Nope. One touch of that and I'd lose my hand.

The icon jumped like spitting sparks, screaming. Flames burned a perfect circle around it, scorching the ground, then they stopped. The pitch of its hissing scream rang higher and higher. I slapped my hands over my ears, but it cut through them and kept going, screeching around my mind. My wolf cowered, hiding in a dark corner, but all I could do was stand there and hope it ended soon. I hated feeling so helpless.

A flash of flames engulfed the burnt circle, far up into the tree line. A tower of fire. A moment later, a woman stood in its center, her blue eyes wide as she drank me in and licked her lips.

My wolf ran out of his hiding place and clawed the edges of my mind, begging to be let free, to go to her. But I denied him. Demon or not, whoever could appear after that shit show was not someone to cuddle with.

8

Del

Shit, shit, shit. I glared at the circle of burnt earth around me and breathed in the ashy air. I'd been summoned. Around me, fragrant pine trees rose toward a mountain peak and a pink morning sky. I hadn't come through any portal maker's circle. My stomach sank toward my knees. I wasn't in the Hell dimension anymore either. Had the seer been right? I checked my necklace, and that icon was still there. It couldn't have been used in the spell. My heart pounded and my head spun, the truth before me now: I wasn't all sex demon, and my second icon had called me to Earth.

Turning, I came eye to eye with two of the men I'd been dreaming about: the hard-nosed leader and the warm playboy. After my dreams, I felt like I knew them already, an almost physical line of connection snapping into place between us. I frowned, wondering what that meant, when I was distracted by a warmth flaring in my stomach, overwhelming my worries. I wanted them, and I was *hungry*. I licked my lips, preparing to give them the charm, maybe convince them to find a way back to Hell with me.

Only, the leader was looking at me like I might explode and the other was backing away slowly. How was that possible? I'd turned my charm on high, and they appeared worried, not interested. Yet, these were the men I'd given myself a tease-a-thon dreaming about for days, starving myself of other men.

Great. Perfect. Exactly what I'd hoped for. I crossed my arms under my bust.

That got their attention. A quick flash in their eyes told me they weren't entirely immune to me, at least not physically, and my hunger roared higher. *Need.*

I bit my tongue, yanking myself back from the precipice. My thoughts swirled in my mind. What had I been doing before this? Amma. Clammy fear slid down my spine. Second icon be damned. What was I thinking, letting my hunger take over? They weren't the biggest problem here. I had to get back. For Amma.

I surveyed the ground, looking for my new icon. Where had they hidden it? I didn't see it anywhere. There must be some way to use it to get home, but methods for returning to Hell after being summoned weren't in the demons' handbook. Best practice was to avoid being called in the first place. Like an idiot.

My eyes fell on the two men again. I was going to need help, and I didn't think they'd want to give it. I sighed, shaking my head. Whatever they really thought of me, I'd have to use my charm on them. It was my best weapon to get out of their grasp and back home.

"A woman?" the leader asked with a smirk.

His whole posture commanded respect. I bet no one messed with him, but it just made me want to take him down a peg or two . . . or six.

"No weapons, claws, or red fiery eyes? I'm terrified," he said, raising his hands in a mock helpless move. "Zeke really thought she'd hurt me?"

Made me kind of wish I was a more ferocious type of demon with talons sharp enough to scratch his eyes out.

I looked at the darker-skinned man. His deep brown eyes watched me carefully, but I could feel the interest simmering there. This was a man who knew women, and he'd had his share of fun. A succubus always knew. Besides—my eyes darted to the disrespectful one—I'd feel better seducing someone who knew danger didn't always come marked with a warning sign. More than ready to run my hands over his coppery brown skin and muscled chest, I licked my lips and jutted out my hip.

He didn't inch any closer, but I had to make a move if I was going to make it home to Amma before she panicked. Logically, I knew she'd call Tarzi when she realized I was missing, but Tarzi couldn't coach her through her emerging powers like I could. My sister needed me.

Smiling like I could make the men's steamiest dreams come true, I beckoned the one I'd dubbed a playboy closer. "Hello. Maybe you can help me. I'd love to know where my icon is."

I gripped my necklace, hiding it from their gaze with my fingers. They didn't need to know I had two. Besides, leaving the other one in their hands meant suffering under their control.

He shook his head, and my insides froze. His eyes weren't glazed.

I tried again, hoping it was a momentary blip. "And you?" I looked to the alpha, so full of authority and sheer-minded confidence. I'd love to take his ego down to the humble, sniffling bedrock with my powers and show him how dangerous I really was.

"How the hell should I know?" He turned his back on me, like I could do him no harm, and faced the other man.

Screw charming *him*. My hands clenched, my nails biting into my palms as I seriously considered gouging his eyes out.

"Did you know this would happen, Cooper?" he asked. "And what do I do with her now? I can't stuff her back in the figurine. It disappeared."

Cooper put his hands up flat in an innocent gesture that seemed practiced. "You know how much I risked bringing the icon to you. I wouldn't do that for fun. And if it hadn't burnt hotter than a blowtorch, we could've made it."

"Unless Zeke put you up to all this," the other man snarled.

I didn't get it. The two of them acted like I wasn't even there. My charms hadn't worked on either of the men. Their eyes hadn't glazed even for a moment, and as unhelpful as that was right now, it brought a swell of joy. Maybe I could bring Amma here and she'd have a life without drawing men like a magnet, the opportunity to have a real relationship, maybe even love? Although that was ridiculous. Everyone knew succubi didn't get to love. I bit my lip. But I'd have to test how far this immunity went, and I still needed to work out how to get home.

Slowly, I stepped away from the two arguing men, into the tree line, and was surprised to find I wasn't rooted to the spot like a demon normally would be in a summoning. At least that's what the stories said. I was free, which meant they'd fucked up. A grin spread across my face. I slipped into the shadows of the trees.

That's when the alpha male's head snapped up and his gold-flecked hazel eyes pinned me, his muscles stiffening as he set his shoulders. Pure command in his tone, he said, "Take one more step."

I turned and ran, but he was catching up, far faster than I expected. *Not an ordinary human. What the hell?* I siphoned off my succubus energy to power my run, but my tank was running on empty. I groaned. I hated to even think it, but I should've listened to my mother. If I'd eaten before I left, I would've left the alpha in my dust.

I was running out of time. He was too fast. My second icon had disappeared during the summoning, but I couldn't let them use the one I still had, so I threw it into the trees, hoping they wouldn't spot it in the brush.

The man behind me didn't falter. I had to hope that meant it went unnoticed. And a minute later, my pursuer wrapped muscled arms around my shoulders. With one forceful tug, he yanked me to a stop. My head hit the man's chin. Maybe it was because I was dazed and maybe it was because I was hungry, but his smell sunk into me, coaxing more warmth from my core. I almost moaned but bit my tongue to stop it. I wanted him. This man helped summon me to this world and all I could think about was how he smelled like cool air and hard toffee. What was wrong with me?

I closed my eyes and took a deep breath. I didn't have to let attraction rule me. I wasn't at the mercy of my urges. I'd battled those with Prax. This man should be no problem, whatever he was.

He turned me in his arms, his grip firm, but not quite bruising. I tried not to think about all the ways he could hold me down and have his way with me. But when I looked over his shoulder at Cooper looking on, biting his lip, I knew he was thinking along similar lines. *Damn it.* Hunger didn't normally make me so addled. But these men . . . they got to me in ways no other man had.

The leader leaned over me, his eyes running over my lips, my neck, and his slow smile, the glint of sharp canines, almost broke me.

"Jaxon, what are you doing with her?" Cooper asked, his tone almost a warning.

Jaxon. So that was his name. Even his name was hot with sharp edges. And Cooper's warning . . . was he warming to me? Was this some kind of delayed reaction to my powers?

"I contained her." Jaxon shook his head, snapping out of the moment we'd shared. "I'll take her for now. Work out what to do with her."

I glared at him, daring to assume I'd consent to this. "You say that like I'm a child."

His eyes ran over my curves. "No, you're a problem." His jaw ticked and he glanced at Cooper. "Go back to Zeke. I'll keep her out of view." He shook his head. "Zeke won't hear about what you did—from me."

I frowned. Was Zeke the other man from my dreams, the one that looked identical to this man? The darker, more playful one? And why were they hiding things from each other? Was it something I could use to my advantage? I wasn't sure how I'd find out. My usual tactic of seducing men and making them tell me their secrets wouldn't work here. I'd have to convince them to work with me.

"Thank you," Cooper said, eyeing me. "I'd be out a pack if this got back to him."

Okay, he was almost as bad as Jaxon. The two were treating me like an object, a problem, rather than a person. My jaw tightened.

"Why the hell did either of you summon me when you're so keen to be rid of me?" My tone was sharp, but screw it, I didn't want to be here either.

Jaxon dug his right hand into my arm and nodded for Cooper to get the other. For now, I let them. I couldn't outfight them, charm them, or outrun them, so it wasn't like I had many other options.

"Where are you taking me?" I asked.

"Back to camp," Jaxon said. "Don't worry, we'll take care of you until I work out how to send you back."

Jaxon sighed heavily as if this was just another item on his towering to-do list. Part of me wanted to massage his broad shoulders and help him relax. That tawny skin, browned from hard work under a hot sun, teased me. If I gave him a rub down, he'd fill my needs too. Warmth slid down my spine and I shook myself—hard. *Head in the game, Del.*

Forcing down my wayward libido, I frowned. "You do want to send me back?"

"Of course I do. Why would I want your kind around here?"

I opened my mouth and snapped it shut again. I'd live with his prejudice if it got me what I wanted, but I wasn't just going to wait for him to bully answers out of someone either. I wasn't some fainting damsel in need of rescue. First chance I got, I was busting out of his camp and finding answers of my own.

9

Cooper

The rain pummeled the truck as I drove the back roads between Jaxon's camp and Zeke's, I was unable to get my mind off of the berry wine scent of that demon, her flashing blue eyes and lush curves that called out for me to put my hands on her. I'd wanted to kiss the shit out of her, meeting her fire with my own. My cock was still hard at the thought. Only the tendril of connection I'd felt when she appeared scared the hell out of me. Women were fun, and I always gave as good as I got, but that's all it was—light fun. Cooper Jones didn't do serious, and every woman on this mountain knew that or they were gone. It was better that way.

Lost in my thoughts, I drew into a parking space before glancing up.

Vince was waiting, his jacket's hood up against the thrashing rain that'd plagued my gray drive back to camp. He banged on my truck, slapping the run-off water, and yanked open my door.

"Zeke wants you. Now." He jerked his head toward camp.

Shit. Did Zeke find out I went to Jaxon? I gritted my teeth and squared my shoulders as the rain soaked through my jacket. Whatever he did or didn't know, I'd done the right thing. And if I had to face up to the consequences, so be it. *Gah.* When did this all get so hard?

Part of me missed the old Zeke. The camaraderie of our late-night parties and chasing women and adventure together. Just last month, we'd gone jumping off the waterfalls over in Frank's Gorge—drinking and carrying on enough to scare the tourists. What was the point of life if it wasn't fun?

I pressed my lips together. But that was before this sorcerer had arrived and convinced Zeke he needed to get all serious about revenge. I was starting to wonder why I'd ever chosen Zeke over Jaxon. If I'd wanted to be called on the carpet over every little thing, I'd have stayed under Jaxon's tyrannical rule.

Vince walked ahead of me, and I stared at his flannel-covered back. What had Zeke thought when the demon didn't show up? He blamed me or I wouldn't have been summoned to him. I rubbed my stiffening neck as we stopped in front of Zeke's RV. *On the carpet for Zeke?* He was more like his brother every day. I was screwed.

Vince knocked.

Ten or so wolves sheltered under roofs or trees nearby, pretending to look busy, but I could feel their eyes drifting toward me. My stomach rolled over. Were they there to back him up? How much trouble was I in? None of them gave me a hint, but they had to be out in this freezing rain for a damn good reason.

I forced my worries down as Zeke's door opened. I had to play it cool.

Zeke glanced at me and waved me inside, his face unusually serious.

When I walked in and saw what he'd been hiding in here, I held back a sigh of relief, my clammy skin cooling in an instant. He had Gabriel on his sofa, tied at the wrists and ankles, and that man's glower could darken an angel's halo.

"You captured the sorcerer?" I asked, keeping my voice calm, casual.

Zeke nodded. "Something went wrong with the spell." A growl rumbled through his voice. "The demon didn't turn up. *He* says she got out of the trap he'd set, which doesn't live up to his promise that we'd have total control of the demon. Or his other promise, that he'd told me everything I needed to know about the spell."

Gabriel had held some things back. My eyes flicked toward the bound sorcerer. *What a surprise.* "I see. Does he know how she got out?"

Zeke met my eyes, his lips pressed tight together, his eyes flashing with frustration.

I nodded. Moving the icon did it.

Zeke ran a hand through his hair and looked to my pockets. "Do you have it?" His voice was low, too quiet for the sorcerer's ears.

Think quick, Cooper. Lie without lying. "No. It heated up and exploded."

Zeke frowned, backing up to sit on a bar stool. "Did the woman appear?"

I cast my gaze through the opening to the kitchen area behind him. Jaxon believed Zeke wasn't like him, but their kitchens were the same—spotless. Both of them wanted—no, needed—control, and I was more than happy to let them have it—as long as they didn't use it to kill each other. My shoulders tightened. I had to play my cards right here.

"She did," I said, "but she got away from me."

He groaned.

I could've lied and said she never showed up, but he had ears in town. If he heard rumors about her, that'd do me no good. With the right amount of drink, Jaxon's people could be loose-tongued. I knew that well enough.

"Where did she go?" Zeke asked.

I grimaced. Internally, I apologized to Jaxon. He'd done me a solid, even if he was a jerk about it, and I was about to pay him back with more trouble. "She ran into Jaxon's property. Too many of his wolves were around. I couldn't follow."

Slamming his fist against the countertop, Zeke cursed. "Did she go up the mountain?"

I glanced at the sorcerer, who was looking on with clear interest.

"From what I saw, yes." Maybe if he thought she was with Jaxon and his wolves, he'd drop this. He couldn't win a full-frontal assault without serious help. That's why he'd summoned the demon in the first place.

I continued, "We should wait and see what happens. They won't know what she is. They'll question her and let her go."

And by then I could convince Zeke this whole thing was an awful idea. The woman didn't even seem that dangerous. Hot as hell, but she'd looked somehow lost after speaking to Jaxon and me. Jaxon hadn't planned to use her powers, just send her back where she came from. That was the right thing to do. Then Zeke and I could go back to having fun. I just had to get him to give up this mad obsession.

I ignored the whine my wolf gave at the thought of never seeing the demon again. She wasn't ours; she didn't belong to us. I shoved those thoughts down, forcing myself to pay attention to Zeke's words. This was why I wasn't a bloody alpha—I sucked at game playing.

Zeke shook his head. "I've waited long enough. And if she says the wrong thing . . . if he realizes he can use her . . ." He sighed. "I can't have him taking advantage of this. We need to get her back. Tonight."

"You're going to invade his property to get her back? Are you crazy? She'll be in the middle of his people. There's no way we get in there unseen. And we don't even know for sure where she is!" My breath ran out at the end of this spout, but I had to keep him from tracking her down.

Zeke glared at me, and I ducked my head. Again, I was reminded of my place. But I had to delay this, give Jaxon a chance to mount a defense.

"How about the sorcerer?" I asked. "Can he tell where she is?"

"If he could, I wouldn't be grilling you about the damned icon." Zeke rubbed his eyes and sighed. "What was she like? Do you think she'll work with us?"

"She looked like a normal woman." I couldn't help the grin that rose to my face, remembering the curves I'd itched to run my hands over. What we could have done had we been alone. "A really hot woman."

Her soft strawberry blonde hair and her tight leather clothes, clinging to every curve . . . If she were anyone else, I'd be chasing her for a few evenings of uninterrupted fun. But the connection rang through my mind again. No, I needed to stay as far away from her as possible.

Zeke shook his head even as he grinned. "You never stop looking, do you? Even a demon looks good to you."

I rolled a shoulder. "Whatever she is, I have eyes. You'll see what I mean." If we found her. *Damn.* I shouldn't be encouraging him.

"You weren't scared of her?"

"No." I frowned.

She was as gorgeous as a supermodel, but she didn't have a harsh, powerful presence. If anything, she'd looked like we'd caught her off guard. And when she was captured, she'd been furious but also defenseless. She certainly wasn't what I'd expected or wanted—definitely not what I wanted. Why was I even thinking in this direction? She was a demon, not a woman, and she needed to go back where she came from. My wolf snarled, clearly unhappy with these thoughts.

"And she didn't persuade you to do anything? Tempt you into doing what she wanted? Gabriel was sure she'd have free rein outside his trap." He stood and crossed to the couch, eying the bound and gagged sorcerer.

"No . . ." So that *was* what the sorcerer had promised. She had tried to tell us to let her go and help her get back to Hell. Did that normally work for her? Was that why she'd looked so lost? "What kind of demon is she supposed to be?"

"Succubus."

I frowned. She'd certainly tried to charm me and Jaxon, but it hadn't worked. "Are you sure we summoned the right demon?"

Zeke grabbed Gabriel's shoulders, sinking his fingers into the sorcerer's collarbone. "We better have, or Gabriel is going to learn what a wolf's claws feel like." He bared his teeth in a mad grin. "We have all day for me to get the truth out of this bastard."

The sorcerer's eyes widened. "You need me. If we don't re-establish the link with the demon and trap her, we can't control her. She'll never do what you want."

Zeke shrugged. "You say that now, but I'll find out the truth." He knocked my arm. "Want to stay and help?"

My wolf brushed closer to the surface, happy to hurt the sorcerer who had divided my loyalties and upended the fragile peace on the mountain. I'd been aching to get to the bottom of his interest from the day he showed up here. "I'd love to."

10

Del

Jaxon lounged against the gray wall across from me, his eyes half-lidded like he was trying to zone me out. He'd sat in here for the whole day, studying me like I was a puzzle to solve, glaring, and finally ignoring me. Was it some kind of power play?

Because he didn't have to guard me in this concrete box. It didn't even have windows. The floor was swept, not even a leaf or a twig to distract myself with. Old blood stains had sunk into the floor and walls, but all I smelled was bleach as if the whole place had been regularly cleaned. Now it was just me, my shackles, and the alpha.

My gaze trailed over the way his tee shirt clung to the hard muscles of his shoulders and arms. I might have squashed my need for the moment, but I definitely wasn't immune to his charms. I bit my lip. Even if he was immune to mine.

The only reason I knew I'd spent way too long trying to talk to this asshole was because he'd left the door open enough to see the light changing as the sun rose and headed back down again. Why didn't he leave me alone? He must have better things to do. Wasn't he hungry? Though maybe the power play was part of sizing me up and seeing what I could do?

I pulled against the shackles, bolted deep into the wall, making as much noise with the chains as possible. I already knew I couldn't get loose. Even at my full power, these were too heavy duty, but I was not about to be ignored after he summoned me and locked me up. If he was staying, he could talk.

"Did my icon really disappear?"

"For the third time, yes," he muttered, rubbing his head.

Okay, not my most original question, but one-word answers had been his go-to since he put me in here and I was about done with it. Whatever I tried, none of my charm worked. He was as responsive as a boulder. Frustrating him was my next tactic. Hell, did I wish I had some secondary powers when my charm was broken. What was my other side? What kind of demon? There could be some powers there that I could use, if only I knew what they were. I'd never needed a plan B before. It both terrified and excited me. The chance to know how people really felt about me, which in Jaxon's case was apparently intense annoyance.

"And you had to lock me up?" I asked. Hell, if I was going to irritate him.

Jaxon grunted. "You're a demon."

And the implication was that he wasn't letting me near his people. "You don't think if I was going to do something, I'd have done it already?"

"Maybe." His eyes watched me, looking dark and threatening.

"Are you going to guard me all the time?"

He didn't respond, but I desperately wanted an answer. He'd rushed me past the rest of his people when we returned to his ramshackle camp on the mountain, but I'd rather one of them guarded me. I knew my charms didn't work on this rock, but I might have a chance with one of them. If I annoyed him badly enough . . .

"Aren't you tired?"

He snarled, "Tired of your endless questions? Yes."

I rolled my eyes. "You expect me to sit quietly in my chains? What self-respecting women let you lead them?"

He growled and jumped to his feet, his fist raised toward me, his eyes almost glowing in the dim light. Then he shook his head and strode out the door, slamming and locking it behind him.

Oh yeah, that did it.

Without the sunlight, I was plunged into complete darkness, but that didn't bother me. I kept my ears perked, wondering if he'd stomped off in a huff or was still guarding me from outside this box. But the metal door was so thick, it was hard to hear more than a mumble of voices, which wasn't much different than what I'd heard for the last few hours as his people returned to camp from jobs and patrol.

Time passed. I closed my eyes and curled up. It was kind of warm with the door closed, and soon I drifted off and with sleep, dreams.

A starkly lit alley stretched in front of me, the cobbled ground coated in surface rainwater. Cold drips raced down my neck. Shivering, I hunched my shoulders, crossing my arms over my chest. I wasn't dressed for this weather.

Scratches on the stone behind me.

I turned. A large, shaggy wolf growled, his lips turned back from his sharp teeth. Our eyes met, his golden and wild.

I shouldn't run. Predators loved the chase, but he was inching closer.

My skin felt electric, each prickle of rain like a lightning rod. Time slipped past until he was three yards away. His body lowered as if to pounce.

I hauled in a harsh breath and ran for my life. But I couldn't run fast enough. He'd been too close. He was gaining on me. Soon he'd topple me to the ground. Use me as a chew toy. I glanced back at his gnashing teeth and challenged my legs to run faster.

And then a figure appeared in front of me, yanking me to a stop.

The alley was gone. I was in a dark room, much like the cement box

Jaxon had chained me to. And my head felt clearer, more present in the dream. How could . . .

Tarzi. That's who'd yanked me to a stop. I figured the wolf represented Jaxon since he was always growling and grumbly, but what was she doing in my dream? Her outfit was familiar: a long dress and a forest green shawl draped over her shoulders.

Chestnut hair flowed over her shoulders, and her familiar eyes watched me. She gave me a limp smile. "I'm sorry about the nightmare."

I was still panting, the ghost of a stitch in my side. "This is really you?"

"Yes," she said, pulling her shawl closer around herself as if she was cold.

Either the dream was messing with me, or Tarzi could talk to me in a nightmare. She could manipulate dreams but . . . all the way from Hell? "You can reach me all the way out here?"

After all the weird dreams I'd been having lately, I wasn't quite sure what was real and what wasn't anymore. After all, Jaxon and Cooper hadn't recognized me, so they must not have had the same dreams I had.

Tarzi grabbed my arms and stared into my eyes. "Focus. What happened?"

Her hands felt solid on my skin. She really was here. My heart swelled. I was so grateful to see her.

"Del, listen," Tarzi said, her no-nonsense tone telling me to snap out of my daze. "Amma called me, freaking out that you weren't home, wondering if you ran off with some men, and then I couldn't get a hold of you."

My heart sank again. *Amma.* "Is my sister okay?"

Tarzi nodded. "But where's 'out here'? And can you wrap it up?"

So much had happened since we last spoke. I didn't even know where to begin. I grimaced. Best start at the beginning.

"It turns out I *do* have a second icon." And likely a second demon heritage and associated powers, though I had no idea what they could be.

Her eyebrows rose. "Your mother filled you in?"

"Not exactly." I bit my lip. It was way worse than that. "I got summoned."

Tarzi drew back, her eyes boggling. "You're on *Earth*? No wonder you wondered how I could reach you."

"Yeah," I said.

Tarzi was so rarely surprised by anything. In dreams and nightmares, she'd seen all sorts of depravity and madness, but this had her reeling. I could tell by her slow blink, defocused gaze, and the frown marring her fair features.

She shook her head. "We need to get you back. Can you get away? Find your icon? Are they controlling you?"

The rapid-fire questions made my head spin, but I tried to answer them one by one. "The icon disappeared when I got here. The men who summoned me actually want me to go back but they have no idea what they're doing. And I don't think I'm under their control. At least, not in the sense you mean." Physically, I was still chained to a wall.

Tarzi frowned. "Then why do you look even more starved? Don't tell me you're still being picky."

"That's not it." I'd go for almost any man right now.

"Then what?"

"My powers don't work on them."

She snorted. "So you have to do it the hard way? So what? You're hot. What's the problem?"

"The *problem* is that they're the men from my dreams, and I don't think they're interested." And I had to get them to come to *me* since I was chained to this damned wall.

Tarzi rolled a shoulder. "Then get them interested. And fast. Amma made an underling service demon give us free food."

I winced. "Did she mean to?"

"No. She chased after him trying to give him the money."

I rubbed my face. "Is she okay?"

"She's scared, but I'm distracting her for now."

"Thank you. I'll get back as soon as I can." As soon as I retrieved both my icons and figured out how to use them.

Tarzi rubbed my arm. "I'll hold you to that. Talk soon."

Drowsily, I opened my eyes and worked on the stabbing crick in my neck. Sleeping in shackles was not my idea of a comfortable arrangement, and I'd be complaining to Jaxon the first chance I—wait. The door was open. And that shadow leaning against the wall was too short and skinny to be the alpha.

"Hello?" I leaned forward, peering at him.

The man stiffened and backed up, which put him into the moonlight. He was young, barely into manhood. Such an insult. Jaxon really didn't think much of me.

"I'm not supposed to talk to you," he whispered, his eyes darting to me and then away again.

Yet he moved a few paces closer, his eyes fastened to me. Were they . . . glazed?

My heart twisted. Despite my current predicament, I'd been thrilled to find I couldn't affect some humans or whatever these were. My powers seemed to work on this one. My heart sank, and I shook myself. *Get over yourself, Del.* If I was going to get out of here, I needed to charm him.

"What's your name, handsome?" I pushed a little power into the words. I needed to get out of here, but it twisted in my gut, using this young man.

"Austin." His voice lifted at the end as if it was a question, as if he was forgetting his own name.

I had that effect on men. I nibbled on my lip. "I'm Del. And I'm really uncomfortable in these shackles. Do you think you could take a look, see if they're too tight?"

He wavered but advanced another few paces. The closer he got, the more stuck he got in my web.

At arm's reach, he bent over me, holding one arm, then the other. And the moment he looked into my eyes, I had him. Completely.

I shook my arms, jangling the chains. "Do you have a key?"

He took it from his belt and held it up. "Right here."

I licked my lips slowly and smiled. *Good puppy.* "Could you undo my shackles?" I'd pushed every last drop of my charm into him, all the power I had left in the tank. This had to work. And if I got him, he'd be mine until I let him go.

He slotted the key into my left shackle, and I could've shouted in celebration, but I held it together long enough to be freed and then gave him the longest kiss I think that boy had ever had. I pulled as much sexual energy from it as I could. He was too young for me to feel comfortable doing much more, but I needed food if I was going to escape. I'd take it where I could.

Energy shot into my veins like double espressos, and I finally felt more like myself.

I pulled back, wincing when I saw his head lolled on his neck, a grin tucking into both his cheeks. I'd rolled him good.

"You're so beautiful," he whispered.

I patted his arm. "Thank you, handsome. Now, can you tell me where the nearest town is?"

First, I needed to get away from Jaxon. He'd find it hard to grab me again around a lot of people. Then I needed to find out how many people around here could be charmed and use them to work out how to get me home. Someone had to have answers.

"Sure. It's down the mountain. South. I have a car?"

"Perfect." I scrambled to remember his name. "That's great, Austin.

We can go now, yes?"

"Yeah, but we have to be quiet. No one can know I let you out."

"Of course not." I kissed him again for good measure and held his hand, swinging our arms between us. A smile bubbled up to spread across my lips. Exploring might even be fun. "Lead on!"

11

Jaxon

I'd barely had a few hours of sleep when someone crashed into my RV and shook me awake. My wolf bristled and I clenched my fists, red hot anger coursing through me.

At the familiar sight of my second-in-command, I gritted my teeth and forced my wolf and my instincts to back down. Mark didn't deserve a punch to the jaw just because he'd barged in without asking. Not even if my wolf was worried it might've been an intruder.

"What is it?" I grumbled, my voice groggy.

I needed more hours. After the burns from juggling that icon up the mountain and chasing down that demon or whatever she was, I needed to refresh my energy. And get rid of the splitting headache she'd gifted me with all her questions and chain rattling. But my second wouldn't interrupt my rest unless there was something I should deal with.

"Austin's missing," Mark blurted.

I jolted upright. "And the woman?"

"Gone."

"Shit." I gritted my teeth and pulled on clothes. "Anyone see which way they went?"

"No. Patrol was on the other side of the camp. They snuck past them."

I shook my head. How could that woman get the drop on Austin when she was shackled to a wall? She'd tried to get me on her side all day, using every method she could think of to sweet talk or annoy me into doing her bidding. I'd warned Austin not to listen to her, not to talk to her. Hell, to barely look at her. That should've been enough.

Jumping out my RV, I asked, "Why would he let her go?" Austin was normally so responsible, and unlike some of the other young men in the pack, he wasn't girl crazy. That's why I'd trusted him with this job.

My second frowned. "He'd never go against your orders."

"Exactly."

I pinched the bridge of my nose and looked around the deserted camp. Almost everyone was in bed, sleeping. I sighed. I had to do it.

"Wake everyone up. Start a search party. We need to find Austin and our prisoner."

Hopefully before she did anything to that poor boy. I never should've put him on watch, but he'd been so eager to step up, I couldn't say no. I'd watched the woman for hours and she hadn't done a thing more dangerous than talk. He should've been *fine*.

My wolf yowled as I rubbed sleep from my eyes. I felt his anger. Austin was one of my wolves, my pack, and I'd let him down. I had to make it right.

My second ran in and out of houses, tents, and RVs, rousing the whole camp. Group by group, they made their way to me. I briefly explained the situation and organized people into teams with the strict instruction to call for me if they found the woman. If Austin could be swayed, maybe they could, too.

I gritted my teeth at the memory of her overly sweet smile and expectant gaze.

We'd find her. We'd check the camp first, then the mountain, and work our way toward town. Austin was young, but he was strong. She couldn't have forced him to go far.

I pulled out my phone and rang the patrol leader, but they hadn't seen any trace of them further down the mountain, so I told them to keep an eye out and wait for more instructions.

"Jaxon?" Mark asked.

"One second." I dropped the phone from my mouth. "Yes?"

My second's frown was deep, and he shifted his weight from one foot to the other. "Austin's dad says his car is gone."

Shit, not good. She'd had up to an hour in a car. She could be miles away by now. And if she didn't have Austin, I might even say that solved a lot of my problems. But she did. I had to bring him home.

I rubbed my face. "Okay, if they have the car, they have to go toward town before they can go anywhere else." I put the phone back to my face. "Have the patrol search the mountain. Thanks." I clicked the off button and faced Mark. "You and I will check town."

"Just us?"

I nodded. I didn't want to take too many of us to face the demon. I knew she couldn't affect me, but after Austin helped her . . . I didn't want to risk more of my wolves. But if I told Mark that, he'd urge me to bring more people.

"Hardly anywhere will be open at this time. It should be a simple sweep," I said.

"Tup's will be busy."

I squinted as I tried to work out why. "Right. It's karaoke night. Hold on. Let me get my keys."

I went for my bedroom, but Mark stopped me and held up his own set. "We'll take mine. I've had more sleep anyway."

I wanted to argue, but I rubbed my pounding head and growled, "Okay."

We hopped into his truck, and he powered down the mountain at full speed.

I lowered my window, hoping the cool night air would take away some of the sting in my eyes and keep me from the slow blink into sleep. Even with adrenalin and guilt clogging my bloodstream, sleep deprivation was catching up to me.

Mark slowed as we hit the town border. Like I'd thought, most houses were shut up for the night. The streets were empty, a few cats yowling in a territory dispute, but they quickly quieted when they caught a whiff of our wolves.

We barreled down the main street, my head on a swivel, checking each side road as we passed, and then we came to Tup's. The slanted roof leaned over the front porch, and I could smell the beer and ribs. Music pumped through the walls. I motioned for my second to turn into the parking lot. I couldn't see all the cars from the road.

But we'd gone no more than a couple yards in when I spotted Austin's dad's beat up silver jeep.

I jumped out of the car and raced for the door to the bar. Blaring music thrummed through me and bright lights danced for my attention, but the stage was empty and no one was singing. No one was waiting either, or getting drinks.

Everyone, to a person, was dancing on the dance floor to the blaring jukebox, and all the women were missing. Even Tup's wife.

I looked around for Tup to ask what was going on but couldn't find him. Then I spotted my captive *behind* Tup's bar. He'd never allow that. And she was helping herself to bourbon, too.

Crossing my arms, I strode to the entry and barred her way. "What are you doing? And where's Tup?"

She jumped and spun to face me, a frown already in place. "That's the man who told me I couldn't be back here?"

"The man who owns this business, yes," I growled. "You're currently stealing his alcohol."

She waved a hand. "I dealt with him."

My eyebrows shot up, my heart beating faster. "Don't tell me you hurt

74

him." *Please.* I couldn't have that on my conscience. Not that I'd been the one to summon a demon to our mountain. *Damn you, Brother.*

She scoffed. "He's fine. Dancing in the middle of that lot. What's the problem? He could stand to exercise more." She took a long sip of her drink.

I couldn't do anything but stare at her. How did she think she could get away with all this? How had she even done it? Tup was a reasonable person, but even his wife couldn't get him to exercise more than a typical bar shift and he was stingy. He'd never give her free drinks.

"What exactly did you do?" My eyes roved over her leather-clad form. She was good-looking, hot even, but not enough to cause this madness.

She rolled a shoulder. "Charmed them."

That wasn't any normal kind of charm. I gritted my teeth. "Undo it."

"I don't think so." She pushed up onto the bar and slid her body over it onto the main floor, reaching back to grab her drink.

My eyes followed the curve of her hip, wanting to reach out for it. But I shook myself. Was her charm getting to me, too? "You can't stay here!" I yelled, battling the music.

She ignored me, sliding deeper into the crowd, the men around her pressing in from all sides. I tried to get through them to her and faced unusual opposition. People usually moved out of the way when an alpha strolled through. A few men even shoved me, men I'd known for years who would never be so rude. *What alternate reality have I fallen into?*

After a few well-placed shoves of my own, I caught up to her again.

She rolled her eyes. "Do you ever give up?"

"No."

"What do you want?" She sipped more of her drink.

"Where's Austin?"

"Oh, my guard? Don't worry, I didn't lose him. He's here in the crowd somewhere. No worse for wear. If you want him, take him."

"Why bring him here in the first place?"

"Well, I needed someone who knew the area, and he took me to this lovely place, so full of good food and good men." Her eyes sparkled. "I've had a great time getting to know the people of this town. They're much more hospitable than you." She frowned for a moment, and then it was gone, wiped away.

"Well I'm glad to hear you're enjoying yourself. But you can't play with people." She was brimming with magic. I wasn't affected by her charm, but I could feel her power surging around me.

"Oh, but I can. I just can't play with you."

I grabbed her arm. A few splashes of her drink fell to the wooden floor. "Come on. We'll grab Austin and get back to camp."

"No. Shackles aren't my kind of accessory. At least, not when I'm in them against my will." She turned to the men next to her and, with a sultry voice, said, "Excuse me, can someone get this man off me?"

The nearest men on either side of me were lads from the college football team, home to visit family. They grabbed my arms and pulled me backwards, well away from her, until I couldn't even see her anymore. And when I tried arguing with them, reasoning with them, they looked right through me like they were hypnotized. *Damn.* Her charm really did work. That's what she'd been saying. It didn't work on me, but it did on everyone else. And that meant . . .

"Mark! Are you here?" He should've come in by now, but I'd been so swept up arguing with her I'd barely noticed his absence. "Wait outside!"

If he wasn't already in here, I didn't want him falling under her spell. But a few moments later, my heart sank. He was already here, dancing near the back of the crowd. There went my backup. I cursed. What did I do now? I was massively outnumbered.

The college kids took me to the door and pushed me outside, then returned to their party. I hesitated on the doorstep. I could go back in, push through everyone, but I'd have to use my shifter powers and hurt people to have a chance at getting to her and bringing her back with me. And that wasn't fair to these townsfolk. They hadn't signed up for this.

I grabbed my phone and called my patrol leader and then my enforcer, telling them to stay away from town, that I'd handle it. Because the more people I threw at this, the bigger her army would get. I rubbed my forehead. She was a far bigger problem than I'd realized.

12

Del

I had to admit, throwing my power in Jaxon's face was a trip. Having held me hostage in a jail cell with real manacles, he deserved it. And I'd pretended like I loved the whole charade of this charm fest to sell my response. Sadly, the only difference between this party and my parties in Hell was that almost everyone was human, and that meant they gave off less sexual energy for me to devour. But it was enough. After some time in the backroom with some of the more attractive candidates, I was feeling like myself again.

Next on my list would be tracking down the other man present when I was summoned— Cooper—and asking him about Zeke. There was a conflict there, and I was almost certain it had something to do with me being called to Earth. If he had any idea how I could get back to Hell, I had to try him. Most people here fell to my charms, so it was worth a shot.

My heart panged, thinking about Amma dealing with that service demon. The longer I stayed here, the more worked up she'd get. She didn't deal with stress or new situations well. She went around and around things in her mind until she was half crazy with it. And Tarzi . . . I loved her, but she'd just tell Amma to stop thinking about it. Like it was that easy.

The bell above the door rang, and I asked the man nearest me to pick me up, ignoring his hand on my butt as I peered to see if Jaxon had returned.

No, that was Cooper. His warm brown eyes jumped straight to me and stopped. He licked his lips and crossed his arms quickly, shaking himself out of it. Even at full power, he was still resistant to my charms. That quick reaction was his own. That connection that I felt thrumming between us—what was that? I tilted my head, trying to puzzle it out. If he had real attraction, could it be possible that he could develop real feelings? What would that be like? Not that I believed in love, at least for succubi, but affection between lovers—what would that be like?

Smiling, I slunk through the crowd to his side. And there was Jaxon . . .

I snapped my fingers. "I need two guards please." Had Jaxon called Cooper in to help him?

Two well-muscled men jostled to my side. One was a man I'd fully enjoyed earlier, after telling him exactly how to please me when he'd looked confused. How was it that men here didn't know how to please their women?

Jaxon tilted his head, his eyes running over my every curve. Despite being sated, I shivered, warmth uncurling low in my belly. I gritted my teeth, trying to ignore it, but it persisted.

He turned his assessing gaze to the crowd and nodded. "You really are persuasive."

I blinked. That joyful sparkle in his eyes, the way he sidled closer to me . . . Oh, he looked just like Jaxon, but this wasn't him—it was his twin. The darker one from my dreams. And in that moment, my want for him exploded into a firestorm. I knew with absolute certainty that he'd know how to please me. No prompting required.

"And what's your name?" I asked, my heart stuttering. He hadn't been compelled either. These three men—they were dangerous.

He leaned into me, his hand reaching for my cheek and then dropping. "Zeke. You must be my demon."

Zeke. The very person I was looking for. I should've guessed he'd be Jaxon's twin. But I didn't like that possessive look in his eyes. Did he think I was just going to do anything he wanted? Even if that sent a shiver through me, I still didn't like it. "Your demon?"

"I summoned you."

"But can you send me back?" I tried not to sound too desperate, but the edge of my want crept into the words. That was the important thing. Fuck him and his sultry possessiveness. I could tolerate it if it got me what I needed—to get home to my sister.

Zeke nodded. "When you've done what I called you for, yes."

"And what is that exactly?" If it was a quick task, I'd do it. I didn't care about their petty human squabbles. My eyes narrowed. No, not human. Now that I was juiced up, I could taste the magic on them. I'd thought it was just the summoning circle before, or maybe the land—there had seemed to be something in the mountain—but now I knew it was them. Before I thought about it, the words tumbled out. "What are you?"

"Why, we're wolves, darling." Zeke grinned.

I blinked. Werewolves still existed here? All the old stories spoke of the powered races dying out long ago. The human realm had lost its magic. Maybe that had been a ploy to keep demons from coming and hunting it out. I had no interest in other magic, but that couldn't be said for all demonkind.

"Are you still with us?" Zeke growled, his charming facade fading with my distraction.

Cooper snarled. "Give her a minute."

My lip quirked at his defense of me. Maybe our connection had gotten to him too. But it hadn't gotten to Zeke or Jaxon. They both saw me as a tool to be used. I sighed. "What do you need me to do?"

"Remove my brother from his pack. Tell him to step down."

I bit my tongue. If he'd asked me to charm almost anyone else . . . He had to pick one of the few who was resistant to me. "That . . . will be difficult."

His eyes narrowed. "You don't want to help me?"

"I want to get home," I said, my eyes drifting to Cooper and his sad eyes. Did he not want me to go? If only we could explore whatever this was between us. "I'm happy to help if that means leaving this place."

"Then what's the problem?"

"The problem . . ." I stepped into his personal space and ran my fingers down his cheek, his chin, his neck.

He watched my every move, his eyes narrowing in pleasure.

"The problem is that he doesn't bend to my will like he should." I glanced at Cooper, standing awkwardly beside Zeke. "Neither does Cooper. Or you."

Though Zeke was attracted to me. He could barely look away, and it wasn't the cold, calculating look he'd have if he only saw me as a solution to his plans. Like Cooper, he wanted me and still had his own will. Three of them immune to my succubus powers—how was that even possible?

"How does your power work?" he asked.

"I use sexual energy to manipulate people. Charm them."

His hand shot forward, gripping my neck and drawing me tight against him, touching from our chest to our thighs.

I gasped and bit back a moan. I definitely wanted him physically, no matter how I felt about him. But I was in a position of power here. I was charged up, and even if he wasn't under my control, everyone else was. Could I really take a chance and try this? Sex with real interest? My heart thumped against my chest.

"Do you need more energy?" He dipped his head, pressing a kiss to my lips.

My breath flew away on the butterflies rioting through my chest. He tasted like sweet bourbon. His tongue slid against mine, pulling a groan from me. Fire ran from my belly down my legs and I leaned hard into him, his hand on my neck and tight on my waist holding me up more than I was.

The plan was to get out of here, to get back home to Amma, but damn if a delay in his bed didn't sound like a wonderful idea. I looked over his shoulder to Cooper, who was guarding the door with a smirk, his eyes glancing back at us every few seconds. Oh, yes, and he'd *want* to join in.

I grinned as I pulled back from the kiss. I'd finally found men who lusted for me naturally, without my magical influence. And my legs were shaking at the thought of pulling them into bed on my own merit. *Yes.*

I slid my hands around Zeke and squeezed his ass. "Maybe more energy would help."

I doubted it, but I needed Zeke on my side and if he slept with me, that should make manipulating him without my powers easier. I grinned. Tarzi would be so proud.

Again, I glanced at Cooper, at the hungry look in his eyes. I craved him in my bed too, but I wouldn't push it. Zeke would want me alone, and I'd let him have me first. But after, I'd ask for Cooper. Because I wanted them both filling me at once, their eyes clear and engaged. The connection between us sang. *Hell, yes.*

I took Zeke's hand in mine and led him into the backroom. I'd already thrown all the visitor's coats on the floor to make a comfy love nest.

Zeke raised his eyebrows, but the devilish grin when he closed the door behind him made my insides spin.

"Busy night?" he asked.

I shrugged. "Could be busier."

He laughed. "My kind of woman." He advanced on me, his eyes molten. Their hazel depths flickered with flecks of gold.

My feet backed up to the coats, and I almost fell.

He grabbed my hips and pulled me against him, threading his fingers through my hair, tugging with that edge of perfect pain.

I grabbed his shirt and twisted my fist, yanking him back to the nest and to the floor. I pulled his shirt up.

His long eyelashes lowered, and a smile tucked into his cheek with a quick flash of his teeth. He raised his arms overhead, letting me rid him of his shirt.

And he did not disappoint. His chest and abs were firm without being overly worked. I licked my lips. Those broad shoulders and that small waist, the V leading into his jeans . . . I ran my hands down his chest, biting my lip, wanting to trace every muscle with my mouth.

Zeke caught my wrists and held them above my head, the force of it jolting the breath from me. His other hand pulled off my top and skillfully undid my bra in one quick move. My heart thumped against my chest. Under my power, men rarely dominated, but Zeke wasn't under my compulsion. The cool air pricked my skin, but my nipples turned to hard pulsing nubs when I saw the predatory hunger in his eyes. *Damn, that was hot.*

I tried to move my arms, to touch him, but he held me tight and tsked. "Oh no. I'm in control here."

He undid the button on his jeans and pulled down his zipper and the top of his boxers. Then he did the same for me, peeling my leather pants off, each brush of his calloused fingers against my soft skin an unbearable tease. He was so close.

I must've made a noise because he ducked to my ear and whispered, "Sing for me."

He pushed his hand into my lace underwear and swirled around my clit, slowly building that pressure within me.

Breathless, I pushed my hips into him, and he moved away, shaking his head. I'd moved too quickly. He wanted this at his speed. He wanted me completely compliant and . . . I was willing to give it a go. Too many times, the men who came to me under the influence of my charms wanted to make me happy and asked what I wanted. Zeke already knew, and he would give it and more.

In one quick move, he dropped my arms long enough to pull my trousers and underwear down to my knees, and then I was back in his hold. He glanced up at me, his dark hazel eyes meeting mine, so clear and full of personality. Daring me to tell him no. But I didn't want to tell him no. I wanted this.

I rubbed myself against his warm cock, loving its hard presence against my lips. I was brimming with tingly need. He was going to take me with his jeans covering his ass, my leathers down around my knees, and there was something so delicious about that, so bad.

"What was that?" Zeke asked. Again, a flash of his teeth told me he was enjoying this.

"Please."

He grinned and pushed inside me, filling me in one swift move. I was so wet I opened for him straight away, and I felt so wonderfully full.

"Yes, like that. Fuck me."

He grunted and dipped his head to nip at my neck, biting it without breaking the skin. And he held me there, at his mercy, as his cock pumped inside me, each thrust brushing up against the spot that spun my pleasure higher, until I was wavering on the edge of the cliff, his hands tight on my arms, his balls slapping against me. He felt so good. And then he changed his angle, and I tensed, my whole body quivering as I came undone.

And that euphoric, eye-rolling pleasure just kept coursing through me, over and over.

"Oh, shit." He released my hands and pounded into me even faster and then came, deep inside me.

I moaned, so much energy buzzing through my veins I wasn't sure if it was all inside me anymore or seeping out. Fucking him was like plugging into lightning.

"Damn," I gasped, power filling me.

Our breath came fast in the quiet room for a few seconds and then he pulled back, lifting his boxers and jeans back over himself and buttoning up.

I pouted, my insides tingly and sore, but in a good way. I was totally up for another round. Though him covering himself up like that did make me feel dirty in the most exquisite way. Everything with him felt so new. Having someone with agency was way more exciting than I'd hoped for. And far more satisfying.

"You're not leaving already?" I asked, reaching out and stroking him through his jeans.

His eyebrow twitched. "Still hungry?"

I smiled. "I want more, yes."

"Well, I need a minute."

I crossed my arms over my breasts. "Then you watch and let Cooper have me."

Zeke laughed and then stilled. "You're serious?"

"Deadly."

He didn't disappoint me. That shit-eating grin said it all. He was totally up for sharing me. And as much as I'd loved having him, I was glad. Though he'd been an energy shock, I liked having more than one man to deal with at a time.

Zeke put up a finger and waved at the door. "One minute." He stood and opened it, glancing back at me one last time before he stepped out.

Muffled voices went back and forth for a minute or two, and then footsteps came my way. It had to be Cooper.

I stepped out of my clothes. If Cooper was up for this, he had to be okay with sharing too. I felt wanton. I'd had multiple men before, but this was different. My connection to these two men hummed through me, and it felt right to welcome them with intimacy. *Wow.* I didn't think I'd ever experienced real intimacy before. Where both parties knew what they were doing and wanted it. I grinned and lay back on the pile of coats.

Cooper pushed open the door, his eyes moving from the floor, to the love nest, to every inch of my exposed skin. He licked his lips and walked over to me, standing a yard away. The height of him looking down at me made me feel vulnerable and sexy. Whatever he said next would set the scene.

"Zeke said you wanted me, too?" He almost seemed to be asking permission, but that huge bulge in his jeans said he was more than up for the task.

I nodded and raised my arms toward him, inviting him closer. "Is Zeke coming too?"

"Yeah. He had a call to make, but he won't be long."

"Good." I bit my tongue, the thought of them taking me from either side overwhelming. I shivered. "You're wearing too many clothes."

Cooper smiled that sexy slow smile I remembered from my dreams. "You think so, do you?"

"Definitely."

"You didn't mind Zeke having you half-clothed."

"He told you?" I asked, pretending outrage. A delicious shiver ran through me. I shouldn't be enjoying this debauchery this much, but I felt like I'd been freed. I'd spent so much time trying not to expose Amma to my feedings that I hadn't let myself enjoy them. Or—I gave Cooper a side eye—was it just because this was different? Because they knew what we did and wanted it as much as I did?

Cooper laughed. "You love it. You wanted him to tell me everything, just like you wanted me to come in here and see how much you like being taken."

"True." I had nothing to be embarrassed about. Like every woman,

I had my kinks, and like any succubus, I wasn't afraid to admit what I liked. "Are you going to leave me hanging?"

Cooper kicked off his shoes and pulled off his top. He then pushed down his jeans and boxers and stepped out of them. And he was just as gorgeous as Zeke. All smooth brown skin, lean muscle, and a bulging cock, demanding attention.

I pushed up onto my knees.

He walked over to me, his cock bouncing around the level of my nose.

I took him into my mouth, stroking him with my tongue, exploring the length of him.

He moaned and put his hands on the back of my head, pushing me deeper. I pulled him into my throat, loving the feel of being so full. His hand grabbed a fistful of my hair and used it to move me up and down.

Even after all my practice, it was a challenge to deep throat his length, but the rumbles running through him, the way his hands tightened, pulling at my scalp, and the twitch to his cock made my clit jump. My thighs were wet, quivering.

And then the door opened, footsteps walking into the room and stopping while the door stood wide open. I moaned around Cooper's cock. He sucked in breath and slowly glanced over his shoulder.

He nodded to the person behind him and pulled out of my throat. Then Cooper pulled me to my feet.

Over his shoulder I saw Zeke. He'd kicked out of his shoes and lost his clothes, and looking at him head to toe made my breath hitch. They were both so perfect. So strong.

Zeke walked around me. I followed him until Cooper grabbed my chin and wrenched me back to him, stealing a hard kiss. My lips tingled. He pushed inside my mouth, his tongue demanding as much attention as his cock, and then hands circled my waist, another hardness pressing against my ass. Zeke hadn't taken long to be ready at all.

I pulled free of Cooper long enough to ask, "Now?"

Zeke shook his head and pressed kisses down my neck. Each one set off shivers that zinged through me, and I was glad for my men's strong grip because my legs were so damn wobbly.

"Not yet. I want to watch," Zeke whispered.

And yet he was so firm against my ass and so warm, pushing gently into my cheeks, rocking slightly as he held me to him.

Cooper smacked the side of my ass, drawing my attention back to him, and his eyes were fiery. Oh yes, he wanted my full attention. I gave it to him, though Zeke's hands running down my body were a huge distraction. And oh, oh, that felt good. Cooper's hand swirled my clit even as he put my hand on his cock and moved it back and forth, pumping himself. He watched my hand without a hint of a smile, and then he kissed me again, all demanding fire, his tongue pushing into my mouth and claiming what was his.

I kissed him back, moaning as his hand pushed me closer to the edge. And the feel of him, filling my hand, Zeke's stubbly chin nestling into my shoulder, his hand now kneading my breast . . . *Hell.*

"Stop, or I'll come," I moaned against Cooper's lips.

He shook his head the tiniest bit. "That's the idea." He increased the pace of his hand, and I fell into another blinding orgasm, my legs giving out completely, my head rolling back into Zeke's shoulder. Aftershocks shuddered through me as power filled me.

Zeke held me steady, my feet only grazing the floor as his teeth nipped at my earlobe, and then we were moving back to the love nest. He pulled me down with him and slid his hand down between us and between my ass cheeks.

I pulled in a deep breath, a giddy smile rushing over my face. I knew Zeke would know what I liked.

His wet finger slid inside my ass, pushing apart the edges and stretching. He moved his finger in and out as Cooper knelt in front of me, dipping his head to—oh, man, that felt good. His tongue licked around my clit until I felt less sensitive, his fingers pumping into me, and then, like he knew when I was ready, he sucked hard on my clit, and just like that I was back on the ladder to another orgasm.

Cooper pulled back and watched shivers rack through me. He grinned at my moans as Zeke inserted a second finger, then a third. His eyes didn't move from my body. Each sound and flicker of movement was caught and enjoyed, his cock so hard as he watched. He gripped his cock in his hand and started to pump as he watched Zeke stretch me wide. And then something much bigger was brushing up against my tight rosebud. Zeke's cock.

"Ready?" he asked.

"Yes. Please."

He pushed. The head of his cock stretched me so wide, and then he kept coming, filling me to the brim. Deeper, and deeper. He pulled me back against his chest as he ploughed into me, his teeth once more claiming my neck, his hand pinching at my nipples. And then when I felt warm, tingly, and oh so full, he was all the way in.

I opened my heavy eyes to find Cooper. He was already between my legs, positioning his cock at my entrance. He rubbed his head over my lips and caught my eyes as he pushed inside.

I breathed deeply, each inch stretching me so far. And then Cooper started a long, slow fuck. In . . . and out In . . . out. I reached around his shoulders and dug my hands into his back. My mind was completely scattered, each stretch and balls-deep thrust mounting the tensed spring inside me and adding to the electric swirl of energy flowing through my veins.

My heart stuttered as Cooper picked up pace, and then Zeke moved slowly behind me and it was all I could do to hold on as the two of them pushed me up that ladder and threw me over the edge. Hard.

I came harder than I ever had before. I wasn't quite sure I was still on Earth. My eyes had fluttered shut and all I saw were stars. I clenched so hard I would've moved if I wasn't pinned between the two men.

Cooper thrust a few more times, and then his cock pulsed deep inside my pussy. Zeke grabbed my hips and pushed up into my ass, finishing not long after. And all three of us lay there for a few minutes, completely spent.

I watched Cooper as he fell back down and finally pulled open his heavy eyes and smiled. He'd enjoyed that as much as I had. And I was sure Zeke felt the same.

Energy was still flaring through me, looking for somewhere to settle, but I was so full, in more ways than one. I grinned. That, I would do again in a heartbeat.

13

Cooper

Man, my head was still spinning. Succubus or not, she was an amazing fuck. I shook my head, trying not to let my face show how much I'd enjoyed that. She was still a demon, and Zeke would still want to use her, even if we'd fucked her. I blew my breath out through my teeth. I couldn't see that going well.

I did up her bra for her.

She smiled a thanks, and it seemed so intimate. Yeah, we'd just had a threesome, but it was more than that. Being with her had seemed so natural, even in a mad romp like that. And already my wolf and my cock were twitching to take her again. With Zeke, without Zeke—it didn't matter. Damn, but I'd not wanted a woman this bad since I first learned how sex worked.

Zeke stood and headed for the door. "Be back in a sec."

The woman moved to stand, but I stopped her, my hand on her arm. "Thank you." My voice came out raspy and quiet.

She frowned. "What for? Because you don't need to thank me for sex."

I laughed. "No." My smile fell away because this meant more, far more, to me. "Thank you for not ratting me out to Zeke."

"That you worked with Jaxon?"

"Yeah. That."

She shrugged, rubbing her hand over my arm. "I saw how you looked at me like a problem on the mountain. I thought it was me, but after I realized Zeke summoned me and after I saw you sweating standing next to him earlier, I understood I wasn't the problem."

I stroked her cheek, loving how she tried not to lean into me but couldn't resist. She felt this as much as I did. "Thank you anyway."

She smiled and pressed a kiss to my palm, stirring up even more heat. I was stiff as a plank for her. Clever, sexy, and oh so kinky. She was perfect. "What's your name?"

"Del."

I rolled it over in my mouth. It felt silly that I hadn't known it when we'd shared such closeness, but I was glad I knew now. Maybe it was time for this wolf to learn new tricks . . . if I could.

The door opened again. I glanced up and froze. Zeke was back, but he'd brought Gabriel and his wolves.

Del stiffened beneath my touch and scooted away from me and to her feet. "Why did you bring so many people in here?" she asked.

She sounded nervous, and I didn't blame her. I scowled at my alpha. "Zeke, what did you do?"

She glanced at the dozen wolves around Zeke. "Leave us," she said, her voice full of command and power.

I could feel her words' power whip through the air and hit our pack. I was sure they'd do what she wanted, but no one moved. Were they immune, like we were? No, Zeke looked too smug, and he wouldn't have let that damned sorcerer out without a reason.

"You spelled them to be immune to her," I said, feeling like the air had been punched out of me.

Zeke didn't agree or disagree, which basically confirmed it. He'd come back for round two after calling the pack. After arranging all this. I shook my head. He was colder than I'd ever been. To use her so thoroughly and then turn on her, just like that. It was like I didn't even know him anymore.

She must've had the same realization because she'd backed up to a wall, her arms wrapping around herself. "You planned this. You had sex with me to corner me here."

"Well, the sex was good," he said, smirking. "Fantastic, actually."

Her lips parted and she shook her head. "Bastard." Her hands dropped to her sides and clenched into fists, and that fire in her eyes, the power radiating from her . . .

My wolf begged me to flank her, to protect her. All my instincts tugged me her way. I even took one step in that direction before Zeke's glance stopped me cold. My alpha had planned this and our whole pack was here. I couldn't go against him.

Del's eyes jumped to me and narrowed to slits. She could dump me in so much trouble in a sentence, and yet she held back, her jaw so tight her cheek twitched.

My guts writhed and my wolf clawed at my throat. This was wrong, so wrong. She was helping me, and I was dragging her into whatever Zeke would demand of her. Using her. *Shit.* But I didn't have a choice.

"Grab her," Zeke said. "We're taking her back to camp."

I didn't want to do it, but I wouldn't let anyone else put hands on her. She tried to dodge me, but she had nowhere to go and eventually submitted. I picked her up, putting her over my shoulder in a fireman's carry and following Zeke, his wolves, and the sorcerer out the bar.

The people inside were still dancing, the music still running, and I briefly wondered how long it'd take for them to snap out of it.

The demon cried out, kicking against me with her boots.

None of her disciples even turned our way. Gabriel must have hidden her somehow. My wolf snorted. *Magic. Bad magic.*

Then we were outside, a drizzle pattering the parking lot.

The succubus shivered, her skimpy outfit doing nothing to protect her from the early morning wind, but the pack vehicles were waiting. She wouldn't be cold long.

I tucked her into the one Zeke indicated, straightened, and looked around at the packed parking lot, at all the people she'd charmed. She'd make a damned powerful enemy, and I feared I'd put myself in the position to be one by siding with Zeke. My wolf whined and pawed my insides.

14

Jaxon

I watched Cooper and Zeke arrive and barge into the bar as rain trickled down the back of my jacket. I fully expected them to get chucked out or sucked into the demon's group of dancers. I was prepared to laugh my ass off at my brother.

Instead, after some time, they came out with the demon bent over Cooper's broad shoulder, restrained. None of their men seemed to be affected in the least, although the faint smell of sex trailed off of them. I could just barely make it out through the rain.

I was going to have to hunt Cooper down and get him to explain how it was that my brother's wolves avoided her charms. My wolf bristled against my skin. He was ready to hunt, but I needed to play it smart. If Cooper really wanted to help me, he'd tell me what the fuck was going on.

Gritting my teeth, I glared at their trucks as they sped out of the parking lot and onto the main road. They'd be back in Zeke's lair in no time, and the demon was sure to be a problem in his hands, but I didn't have the men to challenge them. And I had other problems to deal with.

I got out my phone and called Lyle, tonight's patrol leader. I'd let him know earlier that I'd found the demon and Austin and I was keeping watch, but I hadn't had time to explain things yet. I rubbed my chin. I didn't much want to do it now, but the wolves should know what we were dealing with.

"Are you bringing them back now?" he asked.

"About that . . ." I rubbed my face and sighed. "We hit a snag. Turns out the demon does have powers. She compelled everyone in Tup's."

"Compelled them how?"

"Like hypnotized them? I don't know. It didn't work on me. And don't ask me why. I wish I damn well knew, because she got to Austin and Mark." The memory of Zeke's wolves prancing in like she was any other woman was infuriating.

"Okay . . . what does that mean?"

"It means they're dancing around the bar like they've been spelled by the fairies to dance until they drop. Can you send a few men? I'm hoping it won't be contagious now she's gone."

"Where did she go? Don't we need to find her?"

"Zeke got her." I sighed.

"That's not good."

"I know it's not good! Just send a few men. We need to get people home. I'll deal with the rest later."

I hung up and glared at the screen, a throbbing headache pulsing through my temples.

Zeke had a way of finding the things and people that most annoyed me, but this demon was on a whole new level. Even with help, how was I going to wrangle all the people inside back to their normal lives? I didn't even know where all of them lived, but I couldn't leave them dancing in Tup's all night. It wasn't their fault they got in the middle of my war with Zeke. Or that Zeke lost his damned mind and summoned a god damn demon!

I rubbed at my eyes and tried barging past the door a few more times.

I had to break the party up. But the college guys who kicked me out the first time were having none of it, and I'd need help to get them out without hurting them.

When the patrol leader arrived with the rest of his crew, I blew out a relieved sigh.

"Lyle, good. Help me deal with this." I set my shoulders and strode toward the entrance again.

Lyle's jaw fell open. "You er . . . weren't kidding, huh?"

I crossed my arms. "You think I'd joke about this when I have two wolves in there?"

His smile slipped and he rolled a shoulder. "Maybe? It sounded insane."

I bit my tongue before I lashed out at him. Standing in torrential rain for the past hour had made me a moody bastard. I forced myself to see it through his eyes. And without seeing what I had, it must have seemed like I'd lost it.

"Just help me get our people out."

He nodded and we grabbed the college guys at the door before they could throw me out again. We handed them off to the rest of the patrol. They zip tied them and sat them down by the outside wall under the roof's ledge, out of the rain.

I glanced between Lyle and the crowded bar. Moment of truth. "I might need to go in alone for the rest. I'm not sure if you'll be affected too."

Lyle shook his head vehemently. "I'm not letting you go in alone."

"And if you join them?"

"Then we'll know if it's contagious. You need to know the limits of this power."

I wanted to argue, to order him to stay outside where he was safe. I didn't want another one of my wolves falling to this strange compulsion, but Zeke might turn this on our pack at any moment. I needed to know what the woman could and couldn't do.

"Fine."

We went back in, and thankfully Lyle stayed glued to my side. We searched the crowd for Austin and Mark and found them both in the center of the crowd, swaying side to side and throwing their hands in the air to the beat.

Lyle blew out his breath in a whistle. "Damn."

I had to agree. As we neared the back room, my wolf howled and I scowled. What had happened here? I opened a door and the smell hit me: sex, and lots of it. My senses took it all in, images of what might have happened running through my mind. I'd wanted to peel those leathers off her, and someone had done so. More than one someone, and two that I knew well—my brother and Cooper. *Dammit.* From how much stronger that demon was after time away from me, it was clear she'd fed on the attention of the people around her. And the last thing we needed was a powered-up demon, even if my dick was hardening just thinking about what they'd done. Must be the remnants of her charm. Must be affecting me some small amount. My wolf growled, wanting to be let loose, and I yanked back hard, slamming the door.

"Jaxon?" A wolf from outside was yelling to us.

I stiffened, wondering what else had gone wrong tonight. Had the demon told them all to do something else strange if they got outside? "Yeah?"

"These guys are coming to. They seem normal. Should we let them loose?"

I rubbed my forehead. "Stay on guard and let one loose. If he still seems normal, let the other go."

Because if they took themselves home, that'd take a hell of a lot off of my shoulders.

But the silence after my order had me gnashing my teeth and itching to get back outside. "How's it going out there?"

A long pause. Then . . . "All good. They drove home."

"Great. Did they say what snapped them out of it?"

"They had no idea. But they were beat. All they wanted to do was find their bed. The questions will probably come later."

Ugh. My stomach rolled over. I'd have to talk to the town council about this, and they would *not* be happy my problems were spilling into town. I'd promised them that would never happen. *Fucking Zeke!*

15

Del

The sun had barely peeked over the horizon when a sharp rap at the door caught my attention. I swung my head to face the entrance. Who'd bother knocking when they were checking on a prisoner?

A moment later, a key turned in the caravan's old lock and the door creaked open to show Cooper standing on the step.

I glared at him. "What do *you* want?" They could've at least sent someone who hadn't slept with me to trap me here.

Maybe I'd bit off more than I could chew, wanting men with agency of their own, but I never thought they'd betray me like that. *More fool me.*

Cooper's face fell, his lips turned down as he shoved his hands in his pockets.

Probably a good actor, then. I'd seen him look surprised when Zeke barged into the bar's backroom with their pack, but he had to be in on it. The two of them were close to share a woman so easily, and he'd been distracting me from realizing what was going on outside the room. It was all too neat.

Cooper stiffened as the quiet dragged on, then finally spat out what he came here to say. "Zeke wants to see you."

I sighed. "And you're here to drag me to him?"

"I'm sorry." He met my eyes through his damned thick lashes. "I didn't want to lock you up. What he's doing—it's not right."

Hell, was he a good actor. But his actions didn't back up his words. "If you didn't agree with his plan, you could've said so. But you went along with his every order."

"He's my alpha."

"What does that mean?"

"We're wolves. Werewolves."

"Yeah, Zeke said." I frowned. Despite the magic rolling off them, I hadn't known Earth still had a supernatural community, but some of it must've survived out in the wilderness. I didn't know much about werewolves, but I had heard they had a rigid social order, and the alpha was at the top. But Cooper didn't strike me as a man that backed down. He had power to him, and he was respected by Zeke.

"There's always a choice," I said. And there was more to this issue than he was saying. He defied Zeke once to take my icon to Jaxon. He could've done it again. The risk just wasn't worth the reward to him anymore.

Cooper glanced out the window, his eyes squinting against the bright flare of yellow in the dark sky, the sun just peeking over the horizon. "Come with me."

He stepped out of the caravan, leaving the door open.

I could've stayed on the old sofa cushions and made him haul me out, but what was the point? It'd be better to face this head on. I followed him down the steps and out into the early morning.

The wind was cold, promising autumn was well on its way. I crossed my arms over my chest and rubbed my arms. Hell didn't have this kind of weather, and the tight trousers and skimpy top that felt so comfortable there were highly inadequate here. Not to mention dirty. It was past time I had a change of clothes, but like hell I was going to ask.

Cooper paused. He took in my slight shiver and pulled his sweatshirt over his head. Then he moved to put it over my head.

I backed up fast, my hands up. As much as I'd appreciate the extra warmth, and clothing a little less worn, he was *not* covering my view. Who knew how many of them were hiding in the shadows or what they planned to do with me next?

Sighing, he passed the sweatshirt to me instead. "I'm not trying anything, but I don't want to see you shivering."

He cared, somewhat. Good for him. But I really was chilled. I checked all around for anyone watching before I rolled the sweatshirt so I could get it over my head in one move. *Ugh.* I grimaced. Cooper's smooth vanilla and sandalwood smell that I'd found so attractive the night before clung to the material. Why was it so strangely soothing? He'd betrayed me and captured me for his boss, and I was mooning over his scent. What was wrong with me?

I frowned, realizing I was playing with the cords dangling down from the hood, and shoved my hands into the large front pocket. My cheeks had heated and the shivers were gone, but I wasn't about to thank him. He'd still crossed me, and I was still his prisoner.

He nodded and led the way across the camp, swerving around a large fire tended by a young woman and stopping outside a silver RV that looked much like the rest of the ragtag group of buildings and residences.

Cooper knocked.

The door opened quickly and a man I'd not seen before waved us in, his eyes on me the whole time, narrowed, and suspicious. Oh yeah, these men knew exactly what I could do and were probably pleased for the protection of their damned sorcerer. How they'd found access to someone with so much power on Earth of all places, I had no idea.

The stranger went to grab my arm, but Cooper put up his hand to stop him. "I've got her, Vince."

My eyes darted to Cooper. Why was he doing this? Trying to be nice to the captive? He offered me his hand as I climbed the steps, but I waved him off and walked in under my own steam.

Zeke sat at the small table, cupping a mug of steaming coffee. It smelt strong and bitter, which made me smile despite myself. Seemed like something he'd like.

The sorcerer stood behind him, a menacing presence, his face half shadowed against the wall.

I could've waited to see how this played out, but having Vince at my back and Cooper at my side in the already small RV was making me twitchy. I'd rather cut through the bullshit.

"Why am I here? I hope you don't still want me to work for you, because after the stunt you pulled last night, I really don't feel like it." At the very least, they could've offered me fresh clothes and a shower.

Zeke sipped his coffee, licking his lips as he swallowed, and damn if the bob of his Adam's apple and the waves of steam cupping his cheeks didn't still make me want to wrap my legs around him.

Shit, even the thought of that flared heat inside me, brushing against my skin from underneath. Why was I so drawn to assholes?

"I had hoped you wouldn't see it that way. You're a succubus, no? Sex is like breathing to you."

I frowned but didn't explain how he was wrong. I'd rather not reveal how much last night meant to me, how much I'd wanted to be with men who wanted me for me. And how hurt I was they'd only wanted me for my power after all. Admitting that would give him far too much power and leverage, and I was already at a huge disadvantage without my charm.

"Betrayal is betrayal."

Zeke sat back, his half-lidded eyes looking me over and freezing on the sweatshirt. He glanced at Cooper and raised an eyebrow.

Cooper stiffened but didn't say anything. He *was* helping me more than he'd been told to. He hadn't lied there. And for some reason that warmed me too, made me want to reach out to him and take his hand.

I shook my head. Earth had messed me up big time. I was full of urges and energy I couldn't use to save myself. It was almost as if I cared. I gave a mental laugh. Sure, I loved my sister, but I'd never had feelings for a man. As much as Prax had tried to convince me otherwise, the conniving asshole, succubi didn't get to fall in love.

"I have a deal for you," Zeke said. "Cooper tells me you want to go home, and we filled you with lots of energy last night."

He smirked, and I wanted to punch his nose. How were he and his twin brother both so insufferable in completely different ways?

"I can arrange that, providing you remove my brother for me," he said.

I sighed. Of course he couldn't see how alike he was to his brother. He probably thought he was the better of the two, destined to rule that poor pack. I'd rather a woman took the reins. These two were both addicted to power—wielding it and taking it.

But . . . Amma needed me, and their pack wasn't my concern. But if he still wanted me to remove Jaxon, he was shit out of luck. I could try again with more energy, but I was absolutely certain it wouldn't work. I'd compelled Austin easily enough, so if it'd ever work on Jaxon, it should've worked in that concrete box of a cell.

"I can't do it."

Zeke pushed his drink away, and the scarred one they called Vince crept closer to my back.

My skin bristled, my hair standing on end. I itched to sidestep, put a wall at my back, but that would show weakness and Zeke only respected power.

"You will do it. It's why I summoned you, and my sorcerer assures me it's more than possible. You just need the right motivation."

"No. I can't do it. I was stuck on the mountain with him, and I tried to escape. He can't be charmed."

Zeke waved a hand. "You'll try again now you're juiced up. You said that might help last night. Don't think I forgot."

I gritted my teeth. Even if I admitted that wasn't exactly the truth, he'd bite deep into that white lie because he was so desperate to get his damned way. I'd seen men like him before, so self-assured, so confident they were doing the right thing. And they were so much more frustrating to deal with when I couldn't charm them into believing they were incorrect.

"My powers don't work on you or Cooper or Jaxon. I don't know why, but I know it won't work."

Zeke pushed to his feet, rocking the table and sloshing coffee over the rim of his mug. "You will do what I want if you hope to see home again."

I crossed my arms. "Are you deaf? I'm telling you, if I try this, I'll fail."

Zeke glared at me, and I held his gaze, neither of us backing down. His shoulders hitched up, and he strode two steps closer to me.

Cooper stepped between us, his hand on his alpha's chest and his back inches from my face.

I blinked quickly. Had he just stepped in the way of his alpha to protect me? That didn't make any sense. Why would he do that?

"Get out of my way Cooper," Zeke's voice vibrated through the air with a wolfish growl.

The very air in the room prickled with his power.

I bit my lip. His wolf was so close to the surface. I could feel the energy rolling off him. This couldn't be good. Unlike the human myths, werewolves rarely infected you with bites or scratches, but that didn't mean they couldn't tear me apart.

Cooper didn't move an inch.

I reached for his arm but stopped short of touching him. I felt like these two were kegs of gunpowder. One wrong move and they'd both blow up.

"Perhaps we'd do better finding the icon," the sorcerer said, eying Zeke and Cooper with some suspicion. "If we have that, I can make it so she has no say in the matter."

Cooper and Zeke hadn't stopped their stare-off, but the tension in the room slowly dissolved until Cooper ducked his head.

That made Zeke happy. He swung to face his sorcerer. "Excellent suggestion. Where might we find it?"

The sorcerer frowned. "It should have remained in the earth where I buried it, tied to the trap I'd placed, but . . ." He spread his hands. "It seems to have had a life of its own." His mouth tipped up just enough to tell me he didn't believe that's what had happened.

I didn't either. I went where my icon went, and I'd appeared most of the way up the mountain rather than down here near Zeke's territory. But the sorcerer had a sleek sliminess to his presence I didn't want to get near and helping Zeke would be stupid, even if revealing where I appeared got Cooper into trouble. That icon was my freedom.

"Cooper, take her away. We're done with her for now."

Cooper inclined his head and opened the door.

"And double back after. I need a word."

Cooper muttered something so quiet I couldn't hear him and then proceeded to escort me back to the caravan in complete silence.

He opened the door and gestured for me to go in.

I sunk my hands deeper into his sweatshirt, feeling the super soft lining, and then froze. "You'll want this back." I tugged one arm out of the sleeve.

He shook his head. "You don't even have a blanket. Keep it. I'll come by later with a pillow, a blanket, and something to eat." He turned to go and then looked back. "You're not vegetarian, are you?" He raised his eyebrow like he was sure I wouldn't be.

I almost laughed. "I have no problems eating meat." Then I swallowed hard. Meat. Hell, how did I want him all over again?

Cooper had already shut the door. I waited to hear the twist of the key in the lock. And there it was. Again, I was trapped and alone, but at least I had full use of my arms and a room more comfortable than a concrete box. That was something. But if they got that icon . . . my insides trembled. I might never get home.

I lay on the sofa cushions and shut my eyes, focusing on my breathing and the sounds of the camp. I had to get out of here. I had to absorb as much as I could and look for a way to make a run for it. With enough people around me, neither Jaxon nor Zeke could get to me.

16

Cooper

The camp was quiet after my strategy meeting with Zeke. He'd turned in for the night after we'd spent hours debating how to storm onto Jaxon's property to find the spot where the icon caught fire and disappeared.

My head pounded with the strain of dodging and delaying difficult questions. Trying to keep this conflict from turning into an outright war was becoming impossible. Zeke wanted to take all his fighting wolves onto the mountain to surprise Jaxon's patrol and detain them long enough for him to find the icon. He'd lost the last of his common sense.

Was there some way that Gabriel was influencing him? Magic could do crazy things—could it do that? I hoped not. I was hoping my old friend would come back to me.

I rubbed my face, then unlocked the succubus's caravan and tiptoed up the steps.

There. She had curled up on the sofa cushions, her face hidden in the shadows of my sweatshirt's hood, the hem pulled down over her knees, pushing the fabric out of shape.

My heart melted looking at her like that. Without the skimpy top with full cleavage and half-bare abs, she looked . . . young and defenseless. My wolf howled inside me, demanding I go to her, protect her.

I bit my tongue. I shouldn't be having these kinds of thoughts about a demon. I didn't even have them about the women I regularly hooked up with. But I had promised her a blanket. And after all we'd done, the least I could do was make her comfortable.

I draped the material over her legs and brought it up to the top of her shoulder, then placed the pillow above her head. She'd find it if she woke in the night, but I didn't want to risk her reacting badly to me adjusting her while she slept.

And then I turned to leave, but she turned over and would've fallen off the thin sofa if I hadn't caught her.

She woke, thrashing about, and I held her tight to me.

"It's okay. You fell off the sofa."

She stilled in my arms, her sleepy eyes looking up at me. Then she saw the twisted blanket on the floor. "You came back."

"I promised I would."

She huffed and pulled out of my arms, then settled on the sofa. "I didn't think you'd bother."

I bit my lip. She had no reason to believe anything I said after how Zeke had treated her, and how I had. I'd thrown her to different men from the moment she appeared. My wolf clawed at me, prodding me to say something more, to cheer her up, but where would I even start? I couldn't fix the mess I'd made.

"I . . . I appreciate you not telling Zeke how far up the mountain I was when you arrived."

She sat back. "And who you were with."

I nodded. "I was trying to destroy the icon, make sure a demon didn't come into their fight. If I'd succeeded, maybe you'd still be back home . . ."

Her eyes widened and her hands were rubbing her arms like she was cold, but she wouldn't be in that thick hoodie.

"What is it?" I asked.

"Destroying the icon would've destroyed me. It's linked to my soul."

My throat choked up. I had far more to be sorry for than I'd thought. "It would have killed you?"

"Outright." She glanced at the door and the window. "You won't tell anyone that?" she asked, suddenly realizing what she'd revealed.

"No. That secret is safe with me. I don't want you dead. I want to send you back home." I sat beside her on the sofa cushion and basked in the quiet for a minute, remembering how she'd looked when I first came in compared to how guarded she was now. "You're not like I thought you'd be."

"Not as powerful?" she practically snarled, shuffling a few inches away from me.

"Not as demonic. You're stubborn, sexy, and full of fire, but you're as human as any of us. Though you do enjoy sex more than most." I smiled. It was beautiful to see a woman embrace what she liked as openly as she did.

"Thanks, I think?" She frowned and hesitated before saying, "You know, I dreamed about you before I came here."

"Like about someone like me?" There's no way she could've known me before she was summoned here.

"No. They looked exactly like you. Sitting around a fire like this camp. Zeke was drinking bourbon, his eyes all tactical as he held my icon. Jaxon was surveying his land from the top of the mountain. I saw all your personalities just as they are."

"You're kidding."

"No." She shook her head. "But it doesn't matter. I need to get home." She turned those big eyes onto me, her sharp chin jutted out in challenge. "You want me out of here. Can you make it happen?"

I stroked her cheek before I could think about what I was doing, and she leaned into me before jolting away. There was something between us. A spark. But for so many reasons I couldn't indulge in it. She was leaving, back to her world, and if I didn't get her out of here, she'd be a plaything in Zeke's war.

"I'll get you home. I promise." I rubbed her thigh.

She looked down at my hand until I felt awkward and removed it, but her eyes watched me with something like hope.

"You'd better mean that because it's not just about me. I have people depending on me to get back."

I frowned. "Do you have children?" She had a perfect figure without any sign of stretch marks, but maybe demons didn't get those and she'd definitely said that in the maternal way someone protects their own. My wolf sensed it as much as I did. *Pack.* She had a pack and family waiting for her. Needing her. We had to help her get where she had to be.

"In a way. My little sister is in my care. She's struggling right now, and I wasn't pulled away at the best time."

I nodded, knowing exactly what she meant. My big brother had a pack of his own now, but he'd looked out for me here on the mountain as I grew up, made sure no one hurt me or tried to intimidate me. Since our parents were gone, he'd raised me.

"I understand. I'll do my best." I smiled and stroked her cheek again. This time, she didn't pull away and I leaned in, pressing a soft kiss to her lips.

My heart jumped when she kissed me back. Hell, she brought up things in me I thought were long buried. Everything with her was new and more intense.

I bit my tongue and drew back from her lips before I did something stupid. *Down, Cooper.* I wanted to grab her and kiss her senseless and then do some of those delicious things we'd done earlier, but I caught myself.

She was still our pack's captive, and I wouldn't take advantage. But if

I was to get her out of here, I'd need a plan. The best time was going to be when Zeke and Jaxon were busy with each other, maybe when Zeke was planning this raid, but he'd want me there for that. Sneaking away would be difficult. But I had to make it work. My wolf howled inside me, agreeing. We had to get her home.

17

Del

I felt strangely empty when Cooper left. I'd only known him for a few days. He shouldn't have made such an impression on me. And I'd like to think it was a lack of other people to talk to, but if I was honest it was more than that. In my gut I knew I could trust him. I saw it in how well he took care of me, how he moved between me and his alpha. He wanted to get me out of here, and he'd do a lot to make it happen.

When I pulled the covers over my shoulder and leaned into the pillow that smelt just like Cooper, I thought I'd have good dreams, but I fell straight into a nightmare, two wolves bearing down on me, claws scratching the ground, teeth snapping.

The next moment they were gone and Tarzi stood in their place, signaling for me to stop fighting.

I skidded to a halt and panted to get my breath back. "You really can't visit me without the nightmare?"

"Sorry."

"Right." She at least could've made it about something less relevant, like falling or Prax. But I shook off my misgivings. We had more important things to talk about. "How's Amma?"

My insides knotted. If our mother got wind Amma was alone, she'd be over there in a flash to tug her back to the succubus community. And that was *not* what I wanted for Amma. It wasn't what she needed either, whatever mother said.

"She's fine." Tarzi frowned. "It's more you I'm worried about. Whose top is that?"

I tugged on the sweatshirt, feeling an odd sort of heat in my cheeks. "Cooper's."

Tarzi grinned. "Your cheeks are red. You like him."

I lay my palms against my heated face. I don't think I'd blushed in years. "He's one of the men from the dreams I was having."

"Did you and he . . ?" Her eyes glowed with interest. Forced to see so much horror in people's nightmares, Tarzi loved anything involving pleasure.

"Yes." My core heated at the memories—well, the ones before the betrayal. How could I want these men so much? Even when I was full of power?

"And you wanted to?"

"Yes. It was my choice." I smiled at my friend. I was grateful to have someone in my life that understood me and my struggles with my succubus side.

She grinned. "Was it good?"

I groaned. "So good. But now I'm stuck with his pack. He says he'll get me out, but we have no idea how to get my icon or how to get back home once I have it. The sorcerer is hardly going to help me. He wants me to do everything Zeke says."

"Whoa! Slow down. I'm lost."

I filled her in on everything that'd happened since I was locked up with Jaxon, and she blew out her breath. "You slept with two of them and got an energy jump big enough to blast you into next year. Damn, I wish my sex life was that interesting."

I rolled my eyes. "It's not that great. I'm still trapped here."

"But you have a man on your side. That's something."

"It's something, but it's not ideal. I'd rather get myself out of this." Being a defenseless damsel was not my idea of a good time.

"Well, that'll be hard without people vulnerable to your charm."

Oh, I knew that all too well. Being passed from one pack to the other felt like I was nothing more than a puny service demon. "Can you help at all on your end? Maybe find someone that knows a trick or two to get home?"

"You mean enter the other demons' dreams to mine answers for you?" she asked.

"Yes."

It wasn't like she could reveal to other demons the mess I'd got myself into. They'd see me as weak and, living outside the main community like I did, that'd be nothing but a danger to Amma. And me, once I got back. As much as my powers could do to keep us safe, they didn't work on women or when I was asleep. Or summoned to Earth by annoyingly sexy wolves.

"Fine, but it'll take me ages to work out who to ask, so I better get out of here. Keep that Cooper on your side. He sounds promising."

"Take care of Amma."

"Of course. Talk soon."

She faded from my dream, and my eyes fluttered open in the dark caravan. I heaved in breath and sighed it out, but my chest still felt tight. I had to get home. Amma was more important than another man in my bed.

18

Cooper

I stepped inside the RV. Del sat curled up on the couch, her eyes on the small light coming through the blinds. I set the tray of food down on the counter and crossed to her. I sat on the edge of the couch, reaching for her hands. She let me hold them.

"Are you okay?"

Her lips twisted and she shook her head. "I'm worried about my sister."

I nodded. I'd never felt anything like this before. I was a love and leave them kind of guy, and it was better that way for everyone involved.

She looked up at me from under her thick lashes. "How do you do it?"

"Do what?" I asked, leaning closer. With Del, I just couldn't stop myself from trying to take care of her. I could barely take care of myself, as my brother loved to remind me.

"Put up with them controlling you." She waved her hand toward the window and nibbled on her lip. "Your wolf is just as strong as his."

A faint smile crossed my face. "I've been friends with Zeke—and well, Jaxon too—since I was a pup." Our adventures as young wolves had been legendary—traipsing all over the mountain and pulling pranks. Back then Jaxon had almost had a sense of humor, but Zeke had always been the most fun. The time we got into Mrs. Winthrop's laundry and left her undies in all the logger's pockets . . . A rumble ran through me, but I forced myself back to the here and now.

She rubbed her chin. "Doesn't seem much like friendship."

"Zeke is . . ." I trailed off. "He used to be fun, but since he lost the fight for pack alpha . . . He doesn't like to be pushed around, and Jaxon is demanding . . . harsh sometimes."

"Sure, Jaxon is a jerk." She grinned, an impish glint in her eye. "I don't blame Zeke for wanting to provoke him a bit."

I laughed. "Or a lot."

She unwound her legs, setting her feet on the floor and turning her back to the window. Then her blue eyes met mine. "But I want to know why you put up with it."

I shrugged. "I guess I never cared to run a pack." And a pack wouldn't want to be run by me. Life was too short to do anything but have fun. I rubbed my neck. At least, that's what I'd always thought until I'd met this demon. For some reason, I didn't want to seem less in her eyes, but I still didn't want to be alpha.

Her head tilted. "But why?"

"Not all of us need power to feel happy, Del."

She nodded. "I understand that. I never wanted my succubus power." She pulled the blanket closer around herself.

It must be hard having all that control of men. Every eye looking at you vacantly even as you had sex. I scratched the back of my neck. I'd had my fair share of good times, but every woman I'd been with had wanted to be there and had enjoyed it as much as I had.

"I guess I don't want to be responsible for a whole pack. All those people depending on me. It's not for me."

Del's hand trailed along my leg, and my eyes clung to her movement. She might not be able to roll me, but I certainly wanted her. It didn't feel fair making love when she was trapped here like this, though. I preferred my conquests willing and eager.

"Just-wanna-have-fun-kinda guy, eh?" she asked, scooting closer to me.

"Yeah." A flame burned in the depths of her blue eyes, the fire at its hottest point. I reached for her, pulling her into my arms and kissing her. Heat roared through me, and my cock stood at attention. My wolf whined.

Forcing myself to separate from him, I gained my feet and looked down at her.

"Not such a good-time boy now?" she asked quietly. Hurt crossed her face.

"I—" I licked my lips. "I want you."

Her fingers closed around the fabric of my jeans, and I reached down, untangling them. I couldn't believe I, Cooper Jones, playboy of the year, was turning down what she'd offered, but I was.

"But not like this," I said. "You're a prisoner."

She frowned. "But I'm willing."

"And I'd love to have you when you're free and making your own choices." I gestured to the windows and the camp that lay beyond. "I don't want what we have to be corrupted by this."

Her lips pressed together, but then she nodded. Her eyes swept up to me again. "Can you just hold me?"

"Yes," I said, sitting back down on the couch and taking her in my arms. "That I can do."

* * *

The next morning, Zeke shook me awake. I sat up, covering my yawn. I'd spent most of the night talking to Del like I had for the last week and I'd only just snuck back into my bed. My heart jolted. Had Zeke found me out?

His eyes were set on me, his foot tapping the floor, but he wasn't radiating power and anger like he did when he disciplined the pups.

"Why are you in my room at whatever time this is?" I asked.

"Four."

"Four? Fucking hell." I worked a crick out of my neck. Nothing was worth facing this time in the morning . . . okay, maybe a good woman. That was it. I bit my lip, remembering Del's smooth curves, and then shook the memory from my mind. I couldn't afford to be so distracted around Zeke. He'd sense I was hiding something and get it out of me. "What do you need?"

"We're leaving," he muttered.

"What? To go where?" My feet chilled on the cool linoleum. Autumn was on its way.

Zeke sighed. "To the mountain."

"You're attacking them now?" I rubbed my jaw. It was a good time for it. At this hour, even the patrol would be half asleep, especially knowing they'd be passing off to their replacements at six. "Is everyone ready?"

"Vince is waking them. Gabriel is already in the truck."

"You need to take him with you? Why?" I didn't want to get anywhere near that sorcerer. My wolf howled at the prospect of even smelling his dank magic again.

"For the icon," Zeke said. "He needs to spell it."

Right. He'd want to control Del the moment he found her icon. And I had to do my best to stop him from finding that summoning circle, for me and her. The moment he saw how far up the mountain it was, he'd know I'd taken the icon to Jaxon.

I pushed aside my blanket and slid on clothes, then joined my alpha by the campfire. The crackle and pop of the dwindling flames punctured the lull of the sleeping camp.

Zeke stepped in front of the fire, backlit in red, and went through our action plan for the millionth time.

119

My gaze strayed to the old abandoned caravan Del was locked in. How could I double back and spring her out without being seen? And without allowing Zeke to find the summoning circle. I had to keep him distracted, but no matter how many times I went over it, I wasn't seeing any good options.

I couldn't put Zeke in harm's way to help her. I'd never forgive myself. And if I forewarned Jaxon, he was sure to come down hard on my pack. That was out too. But my wolf dug his claws into my brain and my heart groaned when I thought about leaving Del in camp until her icon was found and she could be controlled like a puppet.

Zeke's speech wound up, and he waved us toward the cars.

I scratched my arm, my gaze fastened on my truck as my sleepy feet took me to the door. No one got in with me. We all had our assigned rides, most of us driving solo in case we got separated on the mountain when dealing with the patrol and had to leave in a rush. I'd convinced Zeke of the need for that at least. And the escape plan would help me if I managed to get away.

Zeke's car spluttered to life and skidded out of the lot. Then Vince's and the other wolves' cars were gone, and in my moment of indecision, I was left alone in the lot.

I bit my tongue. Maybe I didn't have to double back to get Del out of camp. With all our best fighters on the road, we had maybe two men on watch . . . yes. It was the perfect time.

I took my keys out the ignition and shut the door, then jogged into camp. It was still as dead as before, and with only two watchers on patrol, it was easy to slip into Del's caravan without being seen, even easier than it had been the last few days. Then we'd had more people awake around camp.

Del rustled in her blanket, talking in her sleep about needing to get home.

I rubbed her arm.

She blinked awake and froze until she saw it was me. "Hey."

I smiled. "Hey."

Being around her felt so easy. My wolf was already so close to the surface, wanting to nuzzle her neck, but I pushed him down. This wasn't the night for talking about our families and the future. If all went well, we didn't have much of a future anyway. My wolf had to get ready for that.

"Come with me." I left the caravan and waited outside.

A moment later, I heard a thump, a curse, and hurried rustling. She had to be getting dressed in what sounded like record time.

And there she was.

I'd given her some spare clothes, and she was adorable in the overly baggy sweatpants and sweatshirt. My wolf had reared his head again, sniffing the air. She smelled like she was ours. My wolf bared his teeth in his version of a smile. Oh yes, he was far too happy about that. But we couldn't keep her. We were sending her home. Tonight. No matter how much my heart panged at the idea of letting her go.

19

Del

Cooper drove us up the mountain, and each mile the tension in the truck grew until I could almost smell it pressing in on the truck. I scanned the mountainside for trouble, but saw nothing but trees and darkness. Whatever Zeke had planned, it hadn't started yet.

"We're getting close. You need to hide," he said, not taking his eyes off the road.

I raised my eyebrows. "And where do you expect me to do that?"

Cooper gestured to the foot well in the backseat. I opened my mouth to argue, but his brow was creased, his lips downturned as he stared up the mountain. And that worry etched across his normally easy-going face was enough to convince me to clamber into the backseat and roll around on the floor.

But damn was it uncomfortable being banged about with the tight mountain corners and rough roads, doubling back on themselves as we jumped up in elevation. I braced my hands against the seats and my feet against the door, but I'd still see bruises for my trouble.

Cooper checked I was okay after every loud thump, though.

Each time my cheeks heated, and I grew keener to downplay how much

I was getting banged up. He didn't have to care—he wasn't compelled to—but he did anyway. And he'd spent time with me every night he could since I'd been locked up in his pack's camp. Now he was proving he'd meant what he said, that he'd get me out of Earth and back home to Amma. It wasn't right to complain about a few knocks.

My breath hitched, stuck in my swollen throat as I thought about going back to demons who ran at my every whim, obeying my every question. The predictability was nice, but it didn't have the same fuzzy feeling as someone being there for you every night because they wanted to. Leaving Cooper—the only man that had ever been there for me like that— wouldn't be easy.

The truck slowed for a tight corner, and then Cooper put the car into park and switched off the engine. "We're here. Stay down until I come back to the truck."

I didn't dare say anything this close to the rest of the pack, and I couldn't see Cooper from my terrible vantage point, but I heard his door open and felt the weight of the truck shift as he got out and the door slammed shut, vibrating through the floor.

And then I heard the shouts of men nearby, greeting him. They'd probably wondered what took him so long getting here. He said he'd handle that. But still, my heart raced as I waited in the dark. Wondering if he'd be found out. If they'd come for me. If he'd get hurt. He was risking so much, and I'd not even told him how much I appreciated it. Appreciated him.

The men's voices slowly grew quieter until the sounds of the forest took over. Bats, owls, prey, and predators padding through the trees.

Carefully, I sat up, peeking over the sill of the window until I was sure I was alone with the cars. Then I lay across the back seat. No need to be uncomfortable when no one was watching. But should I wait until Cooper got back? I could find the burnt circle where I'd entered this world just as well myself, and it was safer that way, for both of us. It'd also be easier to avoid the goodbye.

I bit my lip. He'd be hurt when he came back and didn't find me, but he'd done his part. I was free out here. And he wanted me gone as much as I did. It was what was best for both of us. He couldn't get in trouble for moving me if I wasn't with him. And that decided it.

I opened the door, but then my ears pricked at running footsteps, and I piled back into the truck, hiding in the footwell and cursing myself for not making a move a minute earlier.

But the running people bypassed the cars, carrying on up the mountain.

I tried again, and this time I saw Cooper, sneaking out from the tree line.

He put his finger to his lips and hurried to my side. "I told you to wait. What are you doing leaving the truck? Jaxon's men are everywhere. It's not safe."

I sighed. "I thought it'd be better for me to leave without your help." I don't know what made me admit it, but I hated how his face closed down, devoid of all the softness I'd come to expect from him.

"I see," he said.

"I'm sorry. I thought . . ."

He shook his head. "It's okay. But I won't let you go alone. There are too many wolves out here for you to make it without my help."

He would hear them coming long before I would—and smell them, too, no doubt. My powers were all too focused in one area. Still . . .

"Are you sure? If they find us, you'll be in so much trouble."

He took my hand in his, smoothing my palm in little circles with his thumb. "You couldn't keep me away."

"Thank you. But the moment you hear a wolf, you're hiding in a tree."

He laughed. "And I'll drag you with me."

We trudged up the steep rocky ground beneath the trees, the rustle of woodland creatures swinging my head one way, then the other. But

Cooper was calm, his eyes set on the path ahead of us. And as our breath synced along the walk, I relaxed into the climb. He'd warn me of any trouble.

I was wondering how much farther we had to go when Cooper grabbed my hand and hauled me off the animal track we'd been following. He hid us behind brambles and held me against him, our faces so close we shared our breath, as thundering wolves powered past us, on the hunt.

When the sounds of the wolves crashing through the undergrowth faded, he let me go, but I felt the tingle of his touch through his sweatshirt and missed the warmth of his hold. In his arms, I'd felt safe. The moment he stepped away, doubts raced back in.

"They didn't smell us?" I asked.

He shook his head. "You smell like me in my clothes, and I'm supposed to be here."

"Oh. So they were Zeke's wolves." I frowned, wondering if Cooper was marking me as his by giving me his clothes, but then I shrugged it off. It didn't matter. I was leaving soon. "Which way?"

He guided me through the forest for another ten minutes, until we were on the edge of the steep slope where I'd got my first glimpse of Earth and the men who'd plagued my dreams.

The burnt circle was still there, the edges as clear-cut and crisp as the day they were scorched into the earth, easy to spot even in the dark of night.

"I guess this is it," I said. My voice was weak. I'd miss him. I stroked his cheek, remembering how he'd done the same for me my first night in camp. And then I pulled the sleeves of his sweatshirt over my hands. "Can I keep this?" I'd meant to offer it back to him, but something deep down didn't want to let it go, to let that last piece of him disappear.

He nodded. "It's yours."

I clenched my teeth, my heart aching. I glanced toward the burnt circle and back to him. All I had to do was go out there and see if I could find my icon in the fiery mess I'd made when I came here, but first . . . I couldn't leave without saying goodbye, without a last taste of a man that helped me because he wanted to, that was attracted to me all on his own, and for more than my looks or my power.

"Thank you, for all you've done to help me."

He nodded but didn't meet my eyes. I couldn't let him go like that, ill feeling and unsaid things between us.

I grabbed the back of his neck and pulled him down to my lips, savoring the sweet taste of him. He nibbled my lip and pulled me tight against his hips so I felt his cock, so ready for me. Wetness soaked my underwear, and thoughts of leaving blew out my mind. I needed him first. Right now. And fast.

I pushed away from him long enough to step out of my sweatpants and shoes and drag his jeans and boxers down. His smile was full of excitement and promise, but when he put his hands on my bare ass and squeezed, all I could do was moan. Something deep inside me grew fiery hot, demanding more of him. *Right. The hell. Now.*

Jumping up, I wrapped my legs around him and laced my hands behind his neck. He positioned himself at my entrance and met my eyes, but I just grinned and sunk onto his firm length in one movement.

He immediately filled me, his head knocking back, a blissful smile spreading across his face, but I didn't give him a moment to enjoy it. A need echoed through me, building and building, and I bounced on him to fulfill it, taking as much of him as I could.

My nails dug into his shoulders, and my mouth tore from his to bite where his neck met his shoulder. He did the same to me, his teeth pinching the skin, and I cried out, muffled but clear. Hell, did he feel good. His scent wrapped around us, sweet and soothing against my skin, his hands hot on my thighs.

"Faster," I panted, sweat slicking down my back.

Being with him again felt so good, so normal. A man—no, a wolf—who wanted me just for me, not for my charm. It was heady and intoxicating. And I'd have wanted to slow down and savor it, if not for the need burning against my skin from the inside, brushing and agitating every nerve, commanding me to see this through.

Stroke after stroke surged into me, hitting that perfect sweet spot until I tumbled over the edge and bit down hard on his shoulder, my insides quivering. He came soon after and sunk us to the ground, our arms still wrapped around each other.

As my breathing returned to normal, I felt more connected to him than I ever had, like a white-hot tether joined us, like whatever happened, I'd never forget him. He was branded into my soul.

I nuzzled into his neck and kissed the bite marks I'd left on his skin. "I'm sorry. That one will probably bruise."

He chuckled, the rumble vibrating through my chest. "Marking me as yours? That's a wolf thing, you know."

I was about to deny it, but something inside me rose up, bristling at the thought of denying he was mine. I frowned. Whatever that was, it wasn't lust. I rubbed my chest. I had to get home, but maybe if I found out how to get there and back, I could visit. I'd ask him to come with me, but his whole family was on Earth. Asking for that would be selfish.

I ran my thumb over the bite mark I'd left, feeling every indent. I met his eyes, searching them for how he felt. They were soft, half-lidded, and he was so relaxed, his arms loosely looped around me. I could wake up every morning like this. But I had to let him go.

I grabbed my clothes and dressed. "You should go. I'm safe now, and your people will be looking for you."

Stiffly, he nodded but didn't leave. "See if you can find the icon first. I won't leave you here if you can't get home."

I didn't want him to risk himself for me, but that feeling inside me was bristling again. And I had no way to force him to go. I found a stick and dug at the burnt circle, feeling around beneath the surface for my icon. I didn't expect to find anything straight away, so I was astonished when, on my second circuit, I felt attracted to a particular spot and the stick hit something hard.

"I think . . ."

I dug into the burnt earth and pulled out my icon. After I dusted off the soil, it looked exactly the same as it had in my dreams, an exact replica of the icon only a few hundred meters away, where I'd thrown it into the trees. But how did I use them to get home? I held it to me, catching Cooper's eyes across the small clearing, and then I squinted. Were those shadows behind him moving?

My heart pounded so hard I felt it pulsing in my ears and, like an idiot, I froze in place, my gaze swinging between Cooper and the shadows. His nose was twitching, and he slowly turned to face the approaching shadows which soon morphed into three men.

Zeke, the sorcerer, and Zeke's enforcer.

I clutched the icon tight and moved it behind my back in a desperate attempt to keep it hidden, but Zeke's dark eyes were already pinned to me and he'd seen the upturned earth in the burnt circle.

How had Cooper not heard or smelt them coming?

"Good job, Cooper." Zeke clapped Cooper on the back.

I must've made a meep of surprise because Zeke grinned and Cooper's face fell.

My heart stuttered. He'd brought me out here for his alpha, and he'd been found out too early. Of course he never wanted to help me. Who was I kidding? No one could really care for a succubus. He just used that excuse as a way to find the icon. Maybe he'd even been here before and knew he couldn't find it without me.

I bit my tongue to keep from yelling at him because it wouldn't do any good. Despite the energy zapping through me, I doubted I could outrun them. Too many wolves were on the mountain. And still, the tether between me and Cooper felt so strong. I felt like it should've crumbled the moment Zeke congratulated him, but I suppose feelings don't die that quickly, damn them. I should've kept to men who couldn't turn their backs on me, and I should've learnt not to trust them the moment Zeke slept with me to get what he wanted.

My nails dug into my icon, and I gritted my teeth. I had to at least try to get out of here. I made a run for it, thrusting every drop of energy I'd gained from that bastard Cooper into stretching my run, injecting more speed.

A curse came behind me and then Zeke yelled, calling his pack to him, and the wolves howled around me, closing in much like they had in my dreams.

I shook off the nightmare and kept moving, toward the parking lot, but it didn't take long for a line of wolves to cut me off, teeth gnashing as they pawed the ground. I couldn't go through them. They'd maul me to the ground and grab the icon from me. I put up my hands, defeated.

The wolves encircled me, and a minute or two later Zeke and his sorcerer descended the steep trail. The sorcerer walked right up to me, protected by the wolves, and snatched the icon from my hands. The glint of sick joy in his eyes was terrifying. With my icon, he could get me to do anything he wanted, anything they wanted, and I already knew I wouldn't like their plans. And what would they do to me when they learned I really could do nothing to Jaxon?

20

Cooper

Most of the pack chased after Del. She was faster than a cheetah with all the extra energy she must've absorbed from me. I hoped she'd get away from them, get back to the truck or hide out somewhere and find her way home. She wouldn't believe that's what I wanted for her anymore, but my wolf pined for her anyway. She shouldn't be tied to Zeke and the sorcerer's will. She should be free. My heart twisted, even though she'd thought I could betray her like that after all I'd done to help her.

Zeke gripped my shirt, twisting the fabric and lifting me onto my toes. "How dare you," he snarled. "I've kept you in my pack; I've let you spout your complaints. And this is how you reward me?" He shook his head. "I should've kicked you out the moment I realized you were strong enough to be an alpha."

He dropped me, a sneer on his lips. "And you helped a demon against me? That's what I don't understand. For her icon to be this far into Jaxon's territory when she came into this world . . ." He stilled. "You worked with Jaxon, didn't you? You went to him for help, and you almost got to the peak to destroy the icon when she arrived."

He scanned my face. I tried to be still as rock, but maybe that was a giveaway in itself because his shoulders slumped.

"You're no wolf of mine," he said. "You're not my pack. Leave my mountain. You no longer have a place here." He spat at my feet.

I backed up a few paces. He was banishing me. I'd reasoned with him, pleaded with him, sided with him, and he was still turning his back on me. My insides iced over. He couldn't do this.

Vince's gaze dropped from me and changed so he looked past my shoulder, and Zeke did the same.

We'd been best friends since we were kids and just like that, Zeke had thrown me away like a seasoned criminal.

"I wanted to help you. This whole plan is insane. You must know that. Your wolf knows it if you don't. You should make peace with your brother. You'll never get back to normal this way." Could he ever understand that me working with Del was me trying to do what was best for him?

"Who said I wanted to get back to normal after what he did? He's the younger brother, and taking my position like that, like he was entitled to it . . . No, you don't deserve an explanation." Zeke waved at Vince. "Escort him back to his truck and make sure he leaves. I can't have him getting in the way of this fight. He's done enough to complicate the situation."

My wolf howled and I felt like saying to hell with this exile. I should beat sense into Zeke, lock him up until he saw reason. But my pack would never allow it. They'd never listen to me now. I may be able to be an alpha, but exile at Zeke's hands would mean I'd never have a place in power here. Helping Del had torn me away from my home. Now I'd have to go to my brother, tail between my legs, and hope he'd let me in.

I bit my tongue hard as emotions raged inside me. Vince and Zeke shouldn't see how much this hurt. Head high, I walked back to my truck. I didn't look back, though I heard Vince trailing me.

When we reached my truck, his steps stopped. I faced him. His wolf was close to the surface, his eyes clear blue and ready to shift.

"Are you going to help him start this war?" I asked.

Vince crossed his arms and nodded toward the truck, still not looking directly at me. Though his jaw was tight. We'd shared more than a few drinks together over the years, but he wouldn't go against his alpha and I couldn't turn the pack against Zeke. So what was left to me but to leave?

I sighed, sunk the key into the ignition, started up the truck, and pulled out onto the road. Vince got in his own truck and followed me to the main road before peeling back to help in the coming attack.

I stared at him in the rear-view mirror until he disappeared behind a corner and gripped the steering wheel hard. How had it come to this? Should I have put my conscience aside and followed my alpha, whatever that meant for Del, Jaxon's pack, or the mountain?

My wolf slashed at me. No, he was right. I'd done the best I could.

21

Jaxon

Mark rushed into camp and skidded to a stop, his head twisting to keep me in sight. "Patrol was attacked."

I opened my mouth and snapped it shut. I didn't need to ask who it was. "When? What happened? How many are hurt?"

"A few cuts and claw marks, but I don't think many were badly hurt. Zeke brought his best wolves. They ambushed us and we fought back hard. We had them on the run. But then the woman we locked up before came. She did something to them. Now our wolves are working for Zeke."

Remembering Tup's, I knew exactly how that had happened. I growled. *Damn demons.*

"She's turned most of the patrol over to their side," Marc continued. "And she's turning more and more as they work their way up here."

I rubbed my face and cursed under my breath. After clearing out Tup's, I was fairly sure that fresh air away from the place they were compelled woke her victims out of their stupor, but she was with them now and they were already in the open air. It didn't seem to be working. We had to get her away from them if we stood a chance of a fair fight. And that meant me getting close enough to peel her away. I was the only one I knew for sure she couldn't compel.

I blew out my breath. "Okay, I need to get to her, remove her from the fight."

It wouldn't be easy if she had my men and Zeke's on her side. I'd have to catch them off guard somehow. "Clear out the camp. Send everyone into town or back to their families. The more people here, the more people she can turn to their side."

"But we'll be leaving the mountain exposed."

My teeth squeaked as I clenched my jaw, a jagged stone falling into my stomach. I'd be leaving the magic inside the mountain without its protectors, but I saw no way around it. "I know. Do it. I'll call you back when she's out of the picture."

Mark ran off, and it was only then I realized he was limping, blood dripping down his leg. Shit, but he must've pushed himself to get here ahead of the attack. I shook my head. I couldn't focus on that now. I had to think about the whole of my pack and what we did next.

I jumped into my RV, unlocked the cabinet in the sleeping area, and took out my handgun, shoving it into the back of my jeans and yanking my flannel shirt over it. I kept it only for emergencies, my wolf preferring more old-fashioned methods of hunting, but this was a damn emergency. If the worst happened and I had to take the demon out, I'd do it. She was a demon, and she'd made her choice. My wolf dipped his head in agreement. Anything for the pack and to protect our mountain.

Peeking through the window of my RV, I saw most of the cars were gone, the last few joining the main road. Doors were left open, swinging in the breeze, and a few things were scattered across the campground, dropped in the rush, but the rest of my people were safe. I smiled grimly. Now for the battle.

I left my RV and headed for the high ground, the tallest part of the mountain. From there I could make sure the mountain's magic wasn't used and I could see where Zeke's men were.

But as I stalked up the almost vertical path, I felt eyes on my back. I dived to the side, my face in the dirt, a moment before a wolf pounced. I twisted and smacked their muzzle, pushing my alpha strength into it, then I hit them a few more times until they were out cold. My heart jumped as I looked them over, but the wolf wasn't one of mine, turned against me. Though that didn't make it much easier. Zeke should never have used his pack this way, for his own damned revenge.

I glanced back down the mountain, keeping low, but didn't see any other wolves. I did see the demon, pacing around the camp, always within a meter of a man my sources told me was Zeke's sorcerer, which was odd. Why would he be so close to her when she was already summoned and on their side?

Looking closer, I saw the demon's movement was strange, delayed and awkward, like she was being pulled against her will through every step. And that's when it clicked. Zeke would never have summoned a demon if he didn't think he could control her. He'd had more than enough time for his sorcerer to fix whatever had been broken when Cooper stole the icon and brought it to me.

I rested my hand on my gun. She wasn't doing this of her own free will. That sucked, but I should take her out anyway. She was a danger to me and mine. My wolf whined. She was ours too. I frowned, shaking myself. There was no way a demon was part of our pack. I took aim. If I just injured her, Zeke wouldn't let that stop her work, and what if I missed? She was surrounded by his—and my—pack. I snarled. I couldn't shoot. I needed to sneak close enough to knock her out, but I didn't know if I could. Keeping her alive made my life a hell of a lot harder. I was one man against an army. How the hell did I get the upper hand?

22

Del

The sorcerer had glued himself to my side, demanding I charm this wolf, check that building, RV, caravan, truck. I was the one in danger, inspecting everything first, and I felt so disposable. I gritted my teeth, one of the few things he hadn't tried to control.

My mind spun through all the things I wanted to do in order to get even with Zeke. I'd go as low and dirty as he had if I had to. Hell, I wanted to. No one deserved a taste of their own medicine more. But . . . was that what this was? Was being controlled like this a first-hand experience of what I'd done to all those men, luring them to my parties, rejecting them or taking them to bed? I bit my tongue. I couldn't think like that. A succubus had to eat and eat well.

"That's all the camp checked," the sorcerer said. He sounded confused.

I was too. I was expecting a bigger fight. I'd turned maybe fifteen wolves to Zeke's side, and they were roaming the mountain, searching for more, but I hadn't heard of any further scuffles. From the size of Jaxon's camp, there should've been dozens.

Zeke strolled in behind us, his chest bare and his lower half clad in jeans and boots. A few claw marks crossed his shoulders. War wounds.

And damn it if I didn't feel my cheeks burn at the sight of him, all that lithe power, fresh out of fighting. Assholes shouldn't look so damn pretty.

"I've got her from here, Gabriel," he said.

"All right."

The sorcerer tossed Zeke my icon like it was nothing more than a toy, and I would've intercepted—it flew right past my nose—but the sorcerer had already commanded me not to try to steal it back. Fighting that spell felt like treading through mud. I got nowhere fast and certainly not quickly enough to snatch my icon from midair.

I blew out my breath as Zeke shoved the icon in his pocket and met my eyes, his sparkling in the moonlight.

"Let's finish up this invasion, hmm? Jaxon has to be hiding around here somewhere. There's no way he'd give me free access to the mountain. I'd bet he's sneaking around, gunning for you."

My stomach jumped, and I stumbled. "He has a gun?"

Zeke nodded. "Oh yeah. He has a few."

I bit my lip. I hadn't thought that in a battle of claws and dominance guns would come into it. It felt like cheating. But then, I wasn't a wolf. And I was already ruining what would've been a fair fight with my powers.

"It's okay, sweet. I won't let him get you." Zeke stroked my arm, like I was a pet.

I recoiled, but he only laughed. And I hated how his warmth lingered on my arm, through the sweatshirt. How could my body still react to him after all he'd done?

"Why are you doing this?" I asked.

"Because Jaxon isn't the right man to protect the mountain's magic. I would've thought that was obvious after tonight."

Obvious to Zeke, maybe. But Jaxon might never have had someone threaten his position if it wasn't for Zeke. Though I wouldn't mention that. I'd already learned that saying things Zeke or the sorcerer disapproved of was highly likely to result in me losing freedoms I currently enjoyed, and I'd need as much opportunity as possible to find a loophole and get out of this.

Without that, my best hope was Jaxon. He'd sent the rest of his wolves away, and he knew I couldn't compel him, so he had one shot to get me out. If he didn't kill me. I shuddered. It was a long shot, and I knew it. The simplest way forward for him was to take me out.

"Oh Jaxooooon! You can stop hiding now." Zeke turned in a large circle, but nothing moved except the wind. "Don't make me set fire to your RV, because I'll do it!"

He'd set fire to his own brother's home? I shook my head. Why the hell had Cooper double-crossed me for this man? Cooper had said he wanted the two brothers to reconnect . . . but then, that was how well he'd played me. He'd pretended to care about me, then he'd abandoned me, leaving me alone to deal with his alpha's demands. *Bastard.*

I sighed as I followed Zeke around the camp, ordered to follow my icon wherever its holder went. I had to find a loophole, before all my options disappeared.

23

Cooper

I blinked and realized I'd been staring at the flash of the white markings in the road and the intermittent streetlights as I got further and further away from the mountain. My mind was numb and cold with regret. I should've done better persuading Zeke away from this course. I should've warned Jaxon about the imminent second attack. Instead I'd led Del into thinking I could help her get away, and I'd failed. Worse, she thought I'd been stringing her along the whole time.

It shouldn't have gone like this. I slapped the steering wheel, gritted my teeth and scrunched up my eyes for a moment, hating everything that'd happened and my own stupid actions. Why had I held onto my loyalty for Zeke for so long?

A loud horn jolted my eyes open. I swerved to avoid a truck coming the other way and cursed. I couldn't carry on driving like this. I had to make a choice. Did I continue driving to the city, search out my brother, and start again, or turn back and make the most of this, despite the fact no one seemed to want me anymore?

My wolf prodded me, pushing forward memories of Del, of how small she'd looked in my sweatshirt, of how pale she'd gone when the sorcerer took hold of her icon. My wolf was so close to the skin, I rumbled with a

139

wolf's growl.

Del was mine, and she needed me. I screeched the tires into a U-turn and turned the truck right back up the mountain, full speed.

I'd have to floor it to get there in time to make any difference, if I even could at all. I'd been too submissive, squishing my instincts and driving away like I was ordered to because I was exiled. But I could be an alpha, too. And it was time to start acting like one.

24

Jaxon

I crept closer to the camp after Zeke and the demon finished their search. They'd checked every building, shadow, and corner, and they hadn't found any more of my wolves. *So far, so good.* Zeke could shout and yell about how he was going to destroy the camp all he wanted—I knew he wouldn't do it. He wanted to move here and take over the pack. He'd never be able to do that if he torched my pack's homes. They wouldn't follow him.

Zeke walked toward the edge of the camp, close to where I hid. No one else was with him except the woman. I extended my wolf senses to be sure, but they were alone. It was now or never.

Bracing in the shadows, I shifted quickly into my wolf form, letting his instincts guide me as I pounced onto Zeke.

He yelled for the demon to charm me off him.

"I can't do that," she said, her face pained at refusing his order.

"Try, damn it!"

Zeke chucked the last of his clothes and shifted to meet me claw for claw. He couldn't give her any more orders, which I hoped would swing the fight in my favor. And so far, it was working. He was underneath me, pushing with his claws, trying to scrabble around into a better position, but I'd got the meat of his shoulder between my teeth and I bit down, drawing blood. It ran down his side as his wolf yelped, unable to keep the pain from coming out verbally. Another minute and I'd have him.

"Jaxon, get off him," she said, more robotic than natural.

And like I expected, her words did nothing. I felt the power in them, the strong aura around her, but they slid off of me like water.

A shot echoed through the camp, and I glanced up, freezing when I saw Vince, my own gun pointed at my snout. He jerked it, signaling me to back off.

There didn't have to be silver in those bullets to kill me. Many werewolves had died over recent years to a "wolf kill". I was outmatched.

Slowly, I released my hold on Zeke and retreated.

"Stop there," Vince said.

I did as ordered, my wolf's tail thrashing from side to side. Zeke had baited me right into another trap, and I hadn't seen it. I hadn't even smelled it. Vince must've hidden behind something pungent, or well upwind, and waited for the right moment to run in. I should've known Zeke would try something like that. This whole invasion had been designed so that I couldn't fight back and win.

Zeke shifted into his human form and pulled on his clothes, barely looking at me. Vince was the one to keep a steady eye on me, never letting up his aim. I didn't have a chance in hell of escaping. They had me, and my wolves couldn't help. I'd failed my pack. I dropped my head and pawed the ground. Whatever happened, I wouldn't submit to Zeke. The mountain didn't deserve him.

"Lock him up in the main cell," Zeke said. "And get a patrol started. This is our territory now."

"What about the girl?" Vince asked.

Zeke frowned as he thought it through, then he chucked the icon to Vince. "Hold her on the other side of the camp. Use the icon to control her and you'll be fine."

And there went any chance of me getting through to the demon. *Great. Fucking perfect.* Zeke finally used his brain and got more consistent, and he used it to overthrow his own brother. My wolf growled. We should've killed him after that alpha fight, twin or not.

25

Cooper

I parked my truck further down the mountain road than I would have liked, just so that I'd have the chance to get in without being noticed. But as I swerved around the parking lot, I didn't like how many of the packs' trucks and cars were still there. Zeke had either won the fight, or it was going on far longer than expected.

Creeping around the main trails, I worked my way toward the camp and climbed a sturdy tree to get a better vantage point. The camp was quiet, the fighting over. It was almost pitch black, but I spotted Vince standing near an RV and one of the other enforcers near the lock up. The obvious place for Del would be the cell but both men appeared to be on guard, their backs rigid with attention.

Sliding down the tree, I moved closer. The RV was on the quieter side of camp, near a clump of tightly packed trees, whereas the lockup was almost in the center of the camp and easily defensible. I'd be totally exposed walking up to it, even in the dark. I had to go for the RV first and hope that checking it didn't reveal my presence.

I swallowed hard and edged around the camp, keeping the RV and Vince in my sight. But as I reached the edge of the tree line to the side of the vehicle and enhanced my vision with the help of my wolf, I spotted a wooden object in Vince's hand. This was it. Del had to be behind that door.

I glanced at the light she'd left on and wondered for a moment if she was okay or injured, scared or still angry at me. Or rather, *and* still angry with me, because that she most certainly was.

My chest felt tight, the bond between us so strong that it tugged me forward, but I pulled against it for another minute. I needed to get my head in order. I couldn't let my wolf and my instincts lead me completely. I needed to use my brain.

How did I get in and take Vince down without anyone else in the camp hearing me? Because that bulge on his belt looked an awful lot like a gun holster and any shot from that would not only be deadly, it'd bring the whole camp down on my head.

I scratched the back of my neck. What I needed was a good distraction, but most of Jaxon's best wolves were here, under Del's influence.

But maybe . . . I grabbed my phone and put in a quick call to Mark, hoping he wasn't one of the wolves Del had turned to Zeke's side. I didn't have many numbers to call.

Mark answered on the second ring, and I blew out my breath. I didn't see any sign of commotion in the camp. He wasn't here.

"Cooper, why are you calling?" he asked.

"I'm on the mountain."

A long pause. "Can you see Jaxon? He hasn't checked in."

"You're not here?"

"No. Jaxon told us all to get the hell out and wait on him."

Sounded like something Jaxon would do. He was always so keen to run into a situation alone and sacrifice himself for his pack. "They're guarding two people. One is probably Jaxon."

"I knew something went wrong! I'll send men up—"

"Wait. You can't barge right in there. Del, the demon, is still here, and she can turn your wolves against each other in an instant. I'm going to get her away. If I manage it, I'll ring you within the hour."

Mark sighed. "That was Jaxon's plan."

"I'll do better."

"I hope so, because if I have to get a sniper up there to take the demon out, I'll do it."

My wolf's hackles rose even as I tightened my hand around the phone. It wasn't an empty threat. Jaxon's pack had more than one link to the military. They loved his no-nonsense rules and rigid pack structure. "Don't you dare."

"She's a demon, Cooper, and it's my pack. I have to get them out, whatever the cost. They'll snap out of it after she's gone."

"You can't kill her."

"Then make it so I don't have to. I'll get everyone in cars now."

I clicked "end" and stared at the phone, knowing I'd burned any remaining links to Zeke, if there were any left. And also knowing my wolf would tear out Mark's throat if he dared murder Del.

Growling, I focused on the RV. I wished I had more time. But with Mark's threat, I'd have to run in and risk it.

My wolf whined, but I growled at him. We'd gotten into this mess, and we needed to get out of it, whatever it took. Right now, that meant taking Del away from Zeke, and getting her somewhere safe.

Deep breath in . . . and out. My nerves were frazzled, but I squared up to the caravan and ditched my clothes, shifting into my wolf. Then I kept to the shadows and upwind. Closer and closer, until I was within easy walking distance of Vince.

His shoulders hunched, and he turned around, looking right at me. He shouted for help, his hand diving for his holster, but I pounced, knocking him to the ground. His head slammed into the side of the RV, clanging in a way that was sure to get people to investigate, but I couldn't back out now.

Vince staggered back to his feet and shifted into his wolf, pouncing on me. I turned and slashed at his side, but he dodged and swiped at my leg. I moaned. He'd cut through something important, and it hurt to put weight on it.

He used my pain to drag me to the floor, pinning me beneath him. I couldn't move. I was going to wind up locked in a room like Jaxon and then Mark would get here and eliminate Del. I couldn't let that happen.

I snapped back at Vince but didn't get more than a few glancing hits in. He had me good.

Breath tore down my throat, every sense heightened. Was that . . . thumping? I tried to look to the RV but couldn't see beyond Vince's mass. But moving about did show me Del's icon, in the middle of Vince's clothes. I dragged us both closer to the wooden item, knowing that was the core of their control over her. If I could get to it, I could shift back long enough to tell her to leave.

One inch, three . . . I stretched my claws all the way out until the wood was in my grasp. The moment I shifted into my human form, Vince's claws would rip into my back, but I had to help Del. I'd heal.

26

Del

I slammed against the metal door of the RV. Cooper had come back for me. When I'd seen a wolf pouncing on Vince, I'd figured it was another fight between Jaxon and Zeke's sides, but then the power of their battle had rolled over me. I knew that scent. Cooper.

The door didn't budge. I pushed on the windows, but I was so weak. My power had been used up turning all Jaxon's wolves and fighting a battle I had no business in, and what I had left was struggling against the restraints they'd put on me through my icon. "Don't use your charm to escape. Do what you're told." The holder of my icon was my power's keeper, and while Vince had dropped it, no one else had broken his commands.

But I had to do something to help Cooper. He'd been the only one who'd helped me, who'd defended me, and he wasn't under my thrall. He'd even come back for me, fighting his own pack. Could it mean that he actually loved me? I blinked. My heart squeezed.

"But love wasn't possible for a succubus." The words tasted like ash on my tongue. My eyes darted to the battle outside. Cooper was hurt, whining. He needed me.

"Dammit, Vince, don't hurt my man." I screamed the words, pounding on the door.

My hand ached from the constant bombardment. I stared at the window centered in the door. If I could break it, I could get out. I could save Cooper. I pulled up all the energy I could, trying to tap into any strength I had. I wrapped a cloth around my hand and hit the window with everything I could muster. Nothing happened.

Cooper was on the ground now, Vince on top of him, snarling.

I growled, the gruff sound erupting from my throat. What the hell was that? I blinked. More than my hand hurt. My heart—no my very bones—began to twist and shorten. I cried out.

What was going on? I tried to think, but I could only feel. *Must get to Cooper. Must save the man I love.* My spine twisted and I screamed. Fur sprouted along my body, and I stared at it, mouth open. Was I somehow a wolf? No, that was wrong. *I am a demon.*

But there was another icon, another power, another form—was I somehow, in my desperation, tapping into it? I cried out again as an agonizing tremor wracked me. I was changing, and what I was changing into was stronger, bigger. I roared.

Pain seared my nerves, but I needed to help Cooper. That was more important. Gathering myself again, I slammed into the door. It shuddered. Hope flickered through me. I roared again.

My vision reddened. Heat curled up my spine as I bent, reforming. The ratty carpet burst into flame. I yelped. Dog-like. Was I a hellhound?

I'd rarely seen one in Hell. Like most demons, they kept to their own. But I knew the stories. Flamed beasts, protectors at best and destroyers at worst. They could shift between human and hellhound forms, but they were strong. And the icon wasn't holding me back. Zeke and his sorcerer must've thought I was all succubus too. They had no idea I had a second form, and their commands didn't prevent me using its power.

I gazed at the door and grinned, though it felt off on my snout. I gathered my strength and charged, slamming against it. The metal creaked and gave. I leapt out, plowing into Vince and rolling him off Cooper. I bit him on the neck, deeper and deeper until blood pooled in my mouth.

Vince shook me off, growling, and I fell back. I pounded him with my paws, and something sizzled. Each place my foot touched, Vince's fur burned away and he was marked with black circles.

Hellhound. My breath caught in my throat. It was fucking amazing.

"Del."

Cooper's voice broke through my daze.

Vince had stopped fighting. He was curled up, whining. I snarled, wanting to end it, end him. He'd hurt my mate. *Fuck.* That made me swallow. *Mate.* I was a succubus, we didn't . . . but hell hounds did. I glanced back at Cooper.

He grinned. "You're fucking fantastic, but don't kill Vince. He was just doing his job."

I growled.

"We've got to go, Del, before they catch us," Cooper said. "Your hellhound form is amazing, but we still can't take on a whole pack."

Why not? I was certain I could take out any number of wolves.

"And a sorcerer," Cooper said. "I have your icon. Let's get out of here."

I nodded.

We took off at an insane pace. I used all the momentum of the steep incline and the power from my four legs to keep up. Four! I huffed, my flames billowing in the wind, my paws burning the ground I ran on. Mother had gotten it wrong. My father was not an incubus, and that had freed me.

But now I had no idea how to turn back. Both the burnt ground under my paws and the light I gave off was a clear indication of our route. Jaxon's wolves I could deal with, but Zeke's were still spelled against me. And I didn't know what powers I had or how strong I was in this form. Although I did break down the metal door. I grinned gleefully.

I glanced up at Cooper. He was breathing heavily. I wished I could ask him how much further to his truck. We'd moved long past the main parking lot we used the first time.

"You need to change back," Cooper gasped. "I'd slow down, but they're close behind us."

I cocked my head, my tail limp, trying to tell him I had no idea where to start.

"Imagine your human body and push your hound into the corner of your mind," he said. "That's how the wolves do it."

I tried doing what he said, but my hound was telling me we were in danger, that I needed all of her speed. I yapped at her. What we needed was stealth. But she wasn't budging.

"We're almost there, okay?" Cooper called.

He'd slowed as we passed through thinning trees. I could see his truck. My hound hopped in the flatbed as he started the engine and peeled out of the lot.

I swung to face behind us, searching for the cars of Zeke's pack, but the road was deserted. And at the speed Cooper was driving, we'd be down the mountain in record time. Had Zeke's wolves all chased us, hoping to cut us off? if so, they'd have to back-track to their cars. Maybe we'd get away.

Cooper peeled around corner after corner, and I scuttled to keep myself from sliding across the metal. I pleaded with my hound that I'd stay on better as a human, that the danger was over, and with a long howl, she relented.

Flames receded beneath my skin, every inch of me feeling like I'd flung myself onto a fire, but I panted through it until I came out the other side, the cool wind of the mountain soothing and chilling my bare skin.

Cooper glanced in the rear-view mirror and yelled over the engine,

"You're back!"

I swallowed against a lump in my throat. "You came back for me, you mean." Tears covered my vision as the emotions of the night caught up to me. He really was on my side.

He grinned. "I wasn't leaving a woman as beautiful as you in Zeke's hands." He slid open the back window and tossed me a blanket.

I laughed, wrapping the flannel around me, and wiped away my tears, but there was still something I had to ask. "Were you working with him to get my icon?"

He gestured to the seat beside him. "No, it's right here and it's yours the moment I can stop and give it to you. Hold on. Next corner's tight."

Did he really mean that? Warmth radiated through me that had nothing to do with the blanket.

I grabbed the side of the truck as we skidded around a hairpin turn and swung onto a much straighter road, coming into the foothills of the mountains, on the road to the city.

After another mile, Cooper pulled over for long enough to give me one of his hoodies and bundle me into the passenger seat. He even tucked the icon into my pocket.

The amber in his eyes was stronger than usual, a sign of his wolf peeking through. "I couldn't leave you. I never could. You should be treated far better than you have."

The bond between us tightened. His hands caught mine, and I closed the distance between our lips. Energy jolted into me more directly than usual, and the beast inside nodded her head in approval. He was ours. And we were his.

Slowly, Cooper pulled back and watched me through his lashes, only breaking the gaze briefly to look at the road behind us.

He straightened, suddenly stiff. "We need to keep moving." He pushed his phone into my hands. "Call Mark. Tell him I got you out."

"Why?"

Cooper grimaced. "You'd rather not know. Just tell him. I'll drive us somewhere safe."

He got back in the driver's side. I squeezed his hand and searched his eyes. There was softness there, but also steel. "Thank you."

"For what?"

"For being the man I always hoped for." For loving me despite my powers and choosing to keep me safe, even above his friends. For so many things that I couldn't even express them all right now, but I was going to show him as soon as we stopped. My core heated as I imagined all the ways I would show him, and I smiled.

* * *

Cooper drove us down into the city. It seemed so huge after the tiny town of Hawkins and the wolves' camps. The roads were busy with different kinds of vehicles and human beings of all sorts. I could feel their energy humming through me again.

We stopped at a small motel on the far side of town and, once we'd booked a room, headed across the street to a diner to refuel. I felt empty, used up after the fight and the running. My eyes ran over Cooper, and I thought of other ways to refuel, but he needed to eat too. So I followed.

The hostess led us to a booth on the far end of the room. Cooper dropped into the seat facing the door, and I gazed out the large window overlooking the parking lot. I rubbed my nose. The crowded restaurant smelled like grease and sweat.

"Do humans always smell like this?" I whispered.

Cooper laughed, the sound rolling out from his chest and making more than a few heads turn. He leaned forward across the table and said, "Yup."

A cloud of perfume came toward us in the form of a woman in a frilly white apron. "Y'all want something?" she asked, tapping her pencil on

153

her notepad.

I snarled, and Cooper squeezed my hand.

"Two farmer specials and two coffees," he said with a smile.

"Hungry boy, ain't ya?" she said, jutting out her hip. Her skirt rode up her legs, and she smiled.

"Yes, we are," he said, gesturing to me.

The woman glanced at me and dismissed me with one look. "Alright, hon. I'll put your order right in."

She strutted away, and I growled, but Cooper just laughed.

"You know I used to be a playboy, but I only have eyes for you now," he said, holding my hand in his. "But I like this new side of you. I'd never imagined a succubus would get jealous."

To be honest, neither had I. I chuckled. There'd been a lot of firsts in the last day or two. My icon now hung around my neck on a makeshift cord I'd found in the truck, close to my heart. Best to keep it where I knew where it was. I'd need to head up the mountain to retrieve my other icon too. I looked at Cooper. I could share this with him. He was on my side now.

"Cooper, I have a second icon for my succubus side. I threw it in the woods when I arrived."

"That's how you have two forms?" he asked. "Succubus and hellhound?"

I nodded, then frowned. "What are we going to do now?"

Cooper looked down at our clasped hands. "I don't know. Everything is such a mess."

I nodded. "And I still need to get back to Amma or bring her here or something, but with the packs fighting and the sorcerer on the loose . . ."

"We need Gabriel to get you home."

"Is that the sorcerer's name?" I asked.

"Yeah," Cooper said, rubbing his temple.

The cloud of perfume came back, and I held my breath while she set down two mugs of coffee and a scattering of cream cups and sugar packets. "Y'all need anything else?"

"No, madam," Cooper said politely.

"Aww, don't call me that," she said jutting her tits out and leaning toward him. "I sound like my momma."

"We're good," I growled. "Go away."

She glared at me, but she moved back down the aisle.

"We need to get the sorcerer without you being caught again," Cooper said, pulling his cell phone out of his pocket. He looked at the screen. "Jaxon was being held there too, wasn't he?"

"Yes," I said. "In the concrete cell."

"I bet his pack would appreciate our help in rescuing him."

I blinked. "I bet they would."

"And you're not being forced to work there anymore, so your charm should be wearing off. It'd be a straight fight."

I shook my head. "But who knows what other tricks the sorcerer has?"

Cooper interlaced his fingers in mine. "We'll face him together."

I was worried about so many things. I needed to catch Tarzi in my dreams and find out what was going on with Amma. Would Jaxon's pack fight alongside us? What new magic would the sorcerer pull out to use against us? But there was one thing I wasn't worried about—Cooper. For the first time in my life, I felt like I had someone I could count on. Someone who would stand by my side and face down our enemies together with me.

I smiled. "We will."

* * *

Can't wait to find out what happens to Del and her men? Read on to learn why hell hath no fury like a demon *scorned* in book two of Hell-Baited

Wolves, Scorned.

ABOUT THE AUTHORS

Cali Mann is the author of the Thornbriar Academy series and Misfit of Thornbriar Academy spinoff series. She writes paranormal romance, the sexy kind with why choose, hunky shifters, sexy vampires, and women who stand up for themselves. She learned romance by reading through her mother's entire Gothic romance collection in her teens so she and dark romance go way back. When she's not writing, she spends her time streaming shows, playing video games, and pestering her two tuxedo cats.

Say hello to Cali online:
www.calimann.com

www.facebook.com/groups/calispack
www.facebook.com/calimannauthor/

Freya Black writes spicy paranormal romance with powerful, kick-ass female leads. Her first exposure to romance fiction was reading hot, contemporary romance published by Mills and Boon. This later morphed into a love for romance with a supernatural twist. Shifters, witches, vampires, aliens, and more are all likely to appear in her books. When not writing, she's often found reading, gaming, and serving her two cats.

Say hello to Freya online:

https://freyablack.wixsite.com/author

http://www.facebook.com/groups/freyaslegion
https://www.facebook.com/FreyaBlackAuthor/

ALSO BY CALI MANN

Thornbriar Academy series
  Found
  Bound
  Saved

Misfit of Thornbriar Academy
  Infiltrate
  Destroy

Blooded Hearts
  Seized

Made in the USA
Columbia, SC
23 July 2023